OUT OF THE BLUE

SEGA®

Facebook: **facebook.com/idwpublishing**
Twitter: **@idwpublishing**
YouTube: **youtube.com/idwpublishing**
Tumblr: **tumblr.idwpublishing.com**
Instagram: **instagram.com/idwpublishing**

ISBN: 978-1-68405-788-7 24 23 22 21 1 2 3 4

COVER ARTIST
ADAM BRYCE THOMAS

LETTERER
SHAWN LEE

SERIES ASSISTANT EDITOR
RILEY FARMER

SERIES EDITOR
DAVID MARIOTTE

COLLECTION EDITORS
ALONZO SIMON
AND ZAC BOONE

COLLECTION DESIGNER
NATHAN WIDICK

Originally published as SONIC THE HEDGEHOG ANNUAL 2020 and SONIC THE HEDGEHOG issues #30–32.

Special thanks to Mai Kiyotaki, Michael Cisneros, Sandra Jo, Sonic Team, and everyone at Sega for their invaluable assistance.

BIG'S BIG ADVENTURE
STORY **IAN FLYNN**
ART **JONATHAN GRAY**
COLORS **REGGIE GRAHAM**

DARKEST HOUR
STORY/ART **EVAN STANLEY**

REFLECTIONS
STORY **CALEB GOELLNER**
PENCILS **AARON HAMMERSTROM**
INKS/COLORS **REGGIE GRAHAM**

EGGMAN'S DAY OFF
STORY **SARAH GRALEY**
PENCILS **LAMAR WELLS**
INKS **BRACARDI CURRY**
& GIGI DUTREIX
COLORS **BRACARDI CURRY**

FLOCK TOGETHER
STORY **SAM KING**
ART **JAMAL PEPPERS**
COLORS **PRISCILLA TRAMONTANO**

THE CATALYST
STORY **GIGI DUTREIX**
ART **ABIGAIL BULMER**

#30–32
STORY **IAN FLYNN**
ART **PRISCILLA TRAMONTANO** (#30)
AND **ADAM BRYCE THOMAS** (#31-32)
COLORS **HEATHER BRECKEL** (#30)
AND **MATT HERMS** (#31-32)

ART BY **YUI KARASUNO OF SONIC TEAM**

BIG'S
BIG ADVENTURE
WOW. WOULD YA LOOK AT THAT?
DON'T MATTER HOW MANY TIMES WE'VE SEEN IT, IT SURE IS PRETTY, HUH, FROGGY?
RIBBIT
THAT TOO!
HAVEN'T BEEN HERE TO SEE IT FOR A WHILE, THOUGH. YOU LED ME ON A PRETTY LONG ADVENTURE...

"FIRST, YOU LED ME ALL THE WAY TO VISTA VIEW..."
VISTA
VIEW SEWERS
TUNNEL SYSTEM
WHAM!!!
HEY, BIG GUY!
HEY, LITTLE GUY.
EXIT
SPANG!
"HEDGEHOG." NOUN. A BURROWING ANIMAL.

"FROM THERE, I FOLLOWED YOU TO RIVERSIDE...
"...TO BARRICADE TOWN..."
LOOKIN' TO SCRAP?
NO.
THEN GET READY TO CRUMBLE!
NO THANK YOU.
"...TO SPIRAL HILL VILLAGE..."
FROGGY! IT'S NOT SAFE HERE! C'MON!
"...BUT I LOST TRACK OF YOU OUTSIDE WINDMILL VILLAGE."

"I SEARCHED HIGH...
"...I SEARCHED LOW...
"I THOUGHT I SAW YOU BOARD THE BIG SHUTTLE, BUT I GUESS IT WAS A WISP INSTEAD. SO I TOOK A NAP.
"I DIDN'T THINK ANYONE WOULD MIND."
I DIDN'T THINK YOU'D BE FOR A BIG TEAM-UP.
SLIDE
SLIDE
I'M HERE FOR MY OWN REASONS.
"WE WENT ALL THE WAY TO ANGEL ISLAND!
"AND YOU'LL NEVER BELIEVE IT FROGGY--IT FELL DOWN! AND I FELL OFF!
?
"BUT IT'S OKAY. IT WENT BACK UP AND I PADDLED BACK TO SHORE TO FIND YOU.
LI'L WATER QUACKER JR.
"IT'S A GOOD THING YOU WEREN'T IN THE OCEAN, 'CAUSE THAT'S A LOOOT OF FISHING GROUND."

"I DECIDED TO RETRACE MY STEPS. I DIDN'T FIND YOU, BUT I *DID* KEEP COMING ACROSS THESE SCARY LOOKING GUYS.
"FIRST THEY GOT VISITED BY A MAGICIAN..."
EGGMAN WILL BE WILLING TO HELP A COUPLE OF MOOKS LIKE US?
I'M SURE OF IT. AS I SAID, I NEED YOUR HELP BRINGING HIM HOME, FIRST.
"...WHO WAS PERFORMING FOR SONIC AND SILVER ON FROZEN PEAK A FEW DAYS LATER.
EGG-
"HE ONLY DID THE ONE TRICK, THOUGH. HE'S A BORING MAGICIAN.
"ANYWAY, THOSE SCARY-LOOKIN' GUYS WERE IN WINDMILL VILLAGE WHEN I GOT BACK THERE.
"I THINK THEIR NAMES WERE... RASH AND TRUFFLES?"
SWING AND A MISS!
"AND I THOUGHT I HEARD THEIR VOICES WHEN I LOOKED FOR YOU IN ECHO MINE, BUT I DIDN'T SEE ANYBODY.
KRAK!
"I GUESS THE LONELINESS WAS PLAYING TRICKS ON ME."

"I WAS STARTING TO GET WORRIED. I COULDN'T FIND YOU *ANYWHERE*...
"...AND THE WORLD WAS GETTING *SPOOKY*. WHOLE CITIES WERE EMPTY.
"I THOUGHT MAYBE YOU'D GONE TO PLAY WITH CREAM, FROGGY. BUT NOBODY WAS HOME!
"I TRIED LOOKING FOR OUR OTHER FRIENDS FOR HELP, BUT I COULDN'T FIND *ANYONE*."

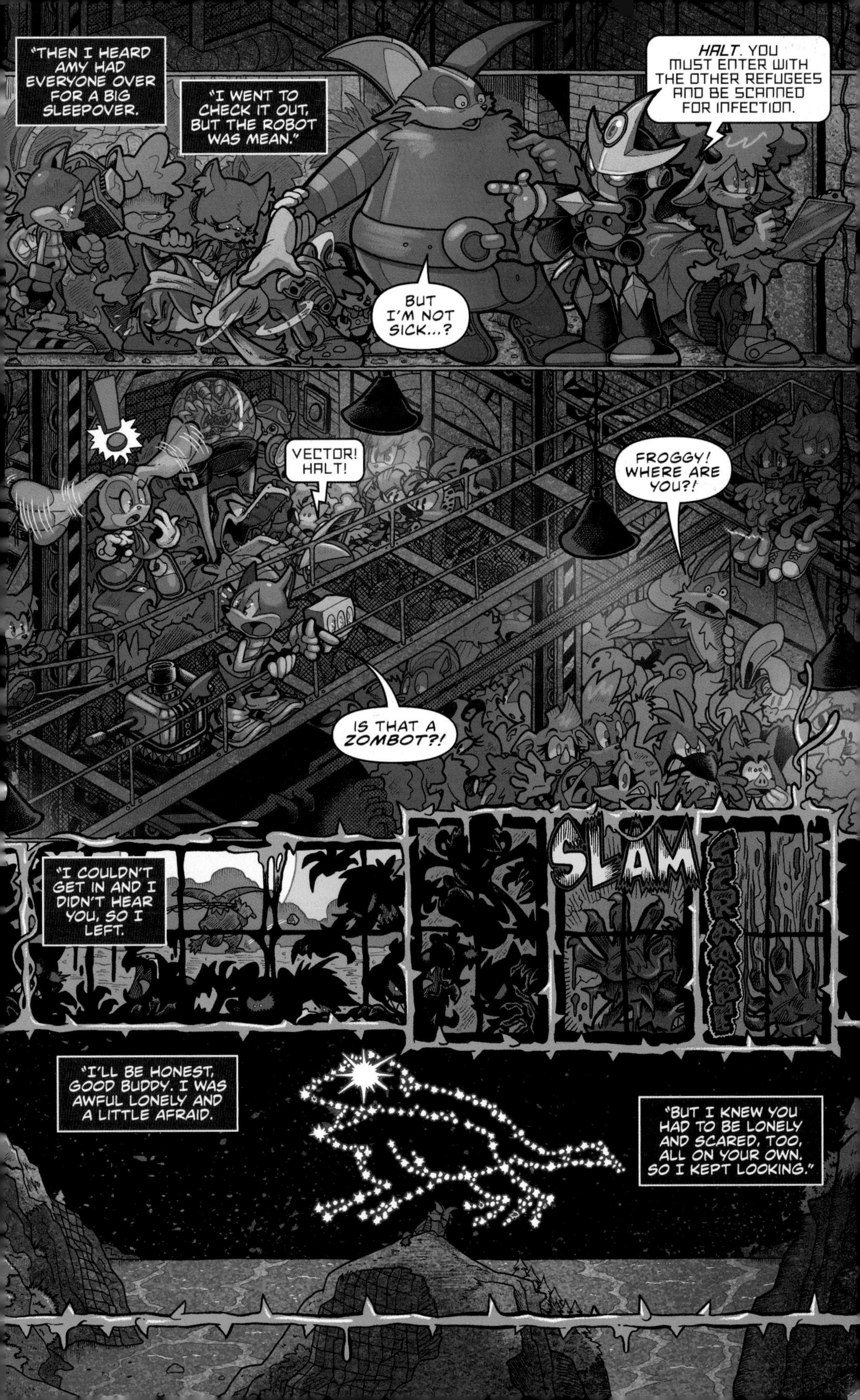

"THEN I HEARD AMY HAD EVERYONE OVER FOR A BIG SLEEPOVER.
"I WENT TO CHECK IT OUT, BUT THE ROBOT WAS MEAN."
HALT. YOU MUST ENTER WITH THE OTHER REFUGEES AND BE SCANNED FOR INFECTION.
BUT I'M NOT SICK...?
VECTOR! HALT!
FROGGY! WHERE ARE YOU?!
IS THAT A ZOMBOT?!
"I COULDN'T GET IN AND I DIDN'T HEAR YOU, SO I LEFT.
SLAM
"I'LL BE HONEST, GOOD BUDDY. I WAS AWFUL LONELY AND A LITTLE AFRAID.
"BUT I KNEW YOU HAD TO BE LONELY AND SCARED, TOO, ALL ON YOUR OWN. SO I KEPT LOOKING."

"I WAS AT THE LAST SPOT TO DOUBLE-CHECK WHEN IT HAPPENED...
TUG
!
"I FOUND YOU!"
I'M SO HAPPY TO HAVE YOU BACK, SAFE AND SOUND! NOW ALL OUR TROUBLES ARE OVER!

"BUT I WAS WRONG. STRANGE MONSTERS WERE ON THE ROAD!"
!
SHING!
I'M NOT GONNA LET YOU GET MY BEST BUDDY!
"AND YOU WERE BRAVE, TOO!
"I MADE SURE THEY COULDN'T FOLLOW US AND WE RAN ALL THE WAY HOME!"

AND YOU KNOW THE REST 'CAUSE... THAT'S IT! WE'RE HOME, SAFE AND SOUND!
YOU MUST BE PRETTY TIRED, 'CAUSE YOU HAVEN'T SAID MUCH SINCE WE GOT BACK.
THAT'S OKAY. WE'RE SUCH GOOD FRIENDS, I KNOW WHAT YOU'RE THINKING.
I'M HAPPY TO BE HOME WITH YOU, TOO.
T H E E N D
FLYNN, JUG! '20

HELLOOOO AND GOOD EVENING! AS ALWAYS, I'M NITE THE OWL AND YOU'RE LISTENING TO K-TBR 199.2: SUNSET CITY'S NUMBER-ONE STATION FOR NEWS AND ADVICE!
KTBR 199.2
AND MUSIC, WHEN I'M HERE BURNIN' THE MIDNIGHT OIL WITH Y'ALL.
NITE THE OWL: DISC JOCKEY & RADIO GURU
HERE'S SOMETHING TO GET US STARTED-- IT'S ONE'A MY FAVORITES, I'M SURE YOU'LL LOVE IT TOO.
CRUSH40
NITE THE OWL IN DARKEST HOUR
AFTER THAT, I'LL BE TAKIN' CALLS, SO IF YOU'VE GOT ANYTHING WEIGHING YOU DOWN TONIGHT, WHY NOT GIVE NITE A CALL?

DON THE ROOSTER: CUSTODIAN, NOT A NIGHT PERSON.
UGH. ANOTHER NIGHT, ANOTHER MESS TO CLEAN UP...
AW, DONNIE, IT'S NOT SO BAD!
THINK OF IT THIS WAY: YOU'RE PROVIDING A VITAL SERVICE, KEEPING THE STATION IN TIP-TOP SHAPE!
AFTER ALL, WHERE WOULD SUNSET CITY BE WITHOUT MY DULCET TONES RIDING THE AIRWAVES?
A LOT BETTER OFF, I'D THINK.
SPEAKING OF, THERE'S OUR FIRST CALLER...!
HELLOOOO, YOU'RE ON THE AIR! WHAT'S YOUR NAME?
G-GALA... LOOK, SORRY, I DIDN'T KNOW WHO TO CALL, AND I ALWAYS HEAR THIS NUMBER ON MY RADIO.
MUST BE KISMET. WHAT'S ON YOUR MIND TONIGHT, GALA?

I NEED HELP! THERE'S THESE PEOPLE, THEY'RE FOLLOWING ME. THEY LOOK SICK...
WHAT?

THEIR SKIN, IT'S LIKE... SHINY? LIKE METAL. I-I KNOW HOW IT SOUNDS, BUT--
MISS, TAKE A BREATH. THIS SOUNDS LIKE A JOB FOR THE POLICE, NOT--
I TRIED THAT, THERE'S NO ANSWER!
I THINK THEY FOUND M--
CLICK
WHAT'S GOING ON?
I-I DUNNO, TAKE A LISTEN...
YOU'RE ON THE--
MY SON, HE CAME HOME SICK. I TOOK HIS TEMPERATURE, BUT NOW I'M-- AUGH--
CLICK
H-HELLO?
ROAD BLOCKED, CAN'T GET OUT--
ALL COVERED IN METAL--
I-I THINK IT'S SPREADING--
HELP--
PLEASE, ANYONE--
I DON'T WANT TO BE--
KHXXX
SSSS...
SSSSSSS...

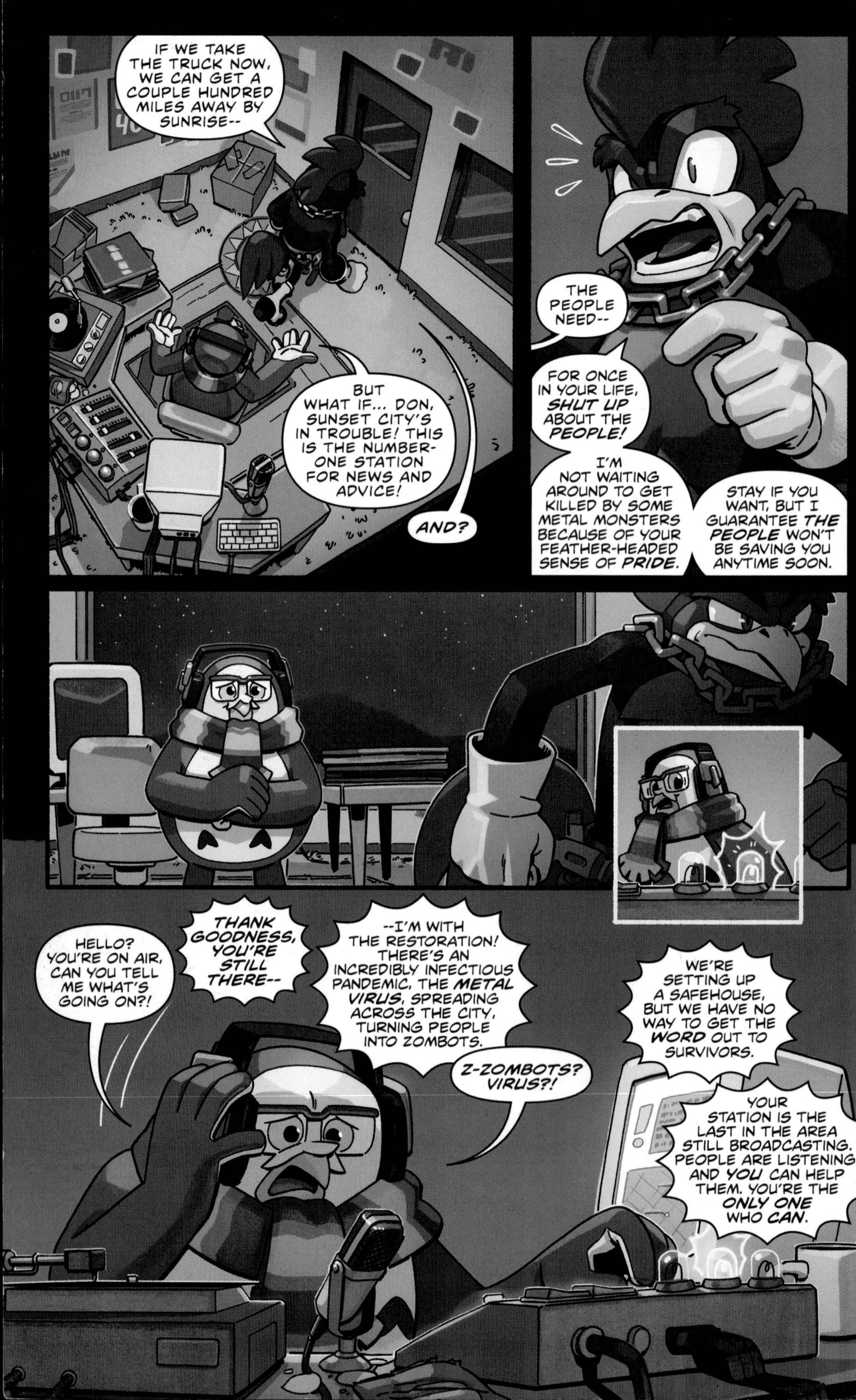
IF WE TAKE THE TRUCK NOW, WE CAN GET A COUPLE HUNDRED MILES AWAY BY SUNRISE--
BUT WHAT IF... DON, SUNSET CITY'S IN TROUBLE! THIS IS THE NUMBER-ONE STATION FOR NEWS AND ADVICE!
AND?
THE PEOPLE NEED--
FOR ONCE IN YOUR LIFE, SHUT UP ABOUT THE PEOPLE!
I'M NOT WAITING AROUND TO GET KILLED BY SOME METAL MONSTERS BECAUSE OF YOUR FEATHER-HEADED SENSE OF PRIDE.
STAY IF YOU WANT, BUT I GUARANTEE THE PEOPLE WON'T BE SAVING YOU ANYTIME SOON.
HELLO? YOU'RE ON AIR, CAN YOU TELL ME WHAT'S GOING ON?!
THANK GOODNESS, YOU'RE STILL THERE--
--I'M WITH THE RESTORATION! THERE'S AN INCREDIBLY INFECTIOUS PANDEMIC, THE METAL VIRUS, SPREADING ACROSS THE CITY, TURNING PEOPLE INTO ZOMBOTS.
Z-ZOMBOTS? VIRUS?!
WE'RE SETTING UP A SAFEHOUSE, BUT WE HAVE NO WAY TO GET THE WORD OUT TO SURVIVORS.
YOUR STATION IS THE LAST IN THE AREA STILL BROADCASTING. PEOPLE ARE LISTENING AND YOU CAN HELP THEM. YOU'RE THE ONLY ONE WHO CAN.

KTBR
199.2
OF ALL THE TIMES... C'MON!
SPRRR-RRR-RR...
...RR-RR-ROAR!
FINALLY!

--YOU THINK ME READING THE RESTORATION'S EMERGENCY INSTRUCTIONS WILL REALLY HELP?
STUBBORN OLD CHATTER-MOUTH...

IT'S THE ONLY CHANCE WE'VE GOT, SIR. WE WOULDN'T ASK IF--
NO, YOU'RE RIGHT. IF EVEN ONE PERSON IS SPARED...
...IT'S WORTH IT TO ME.

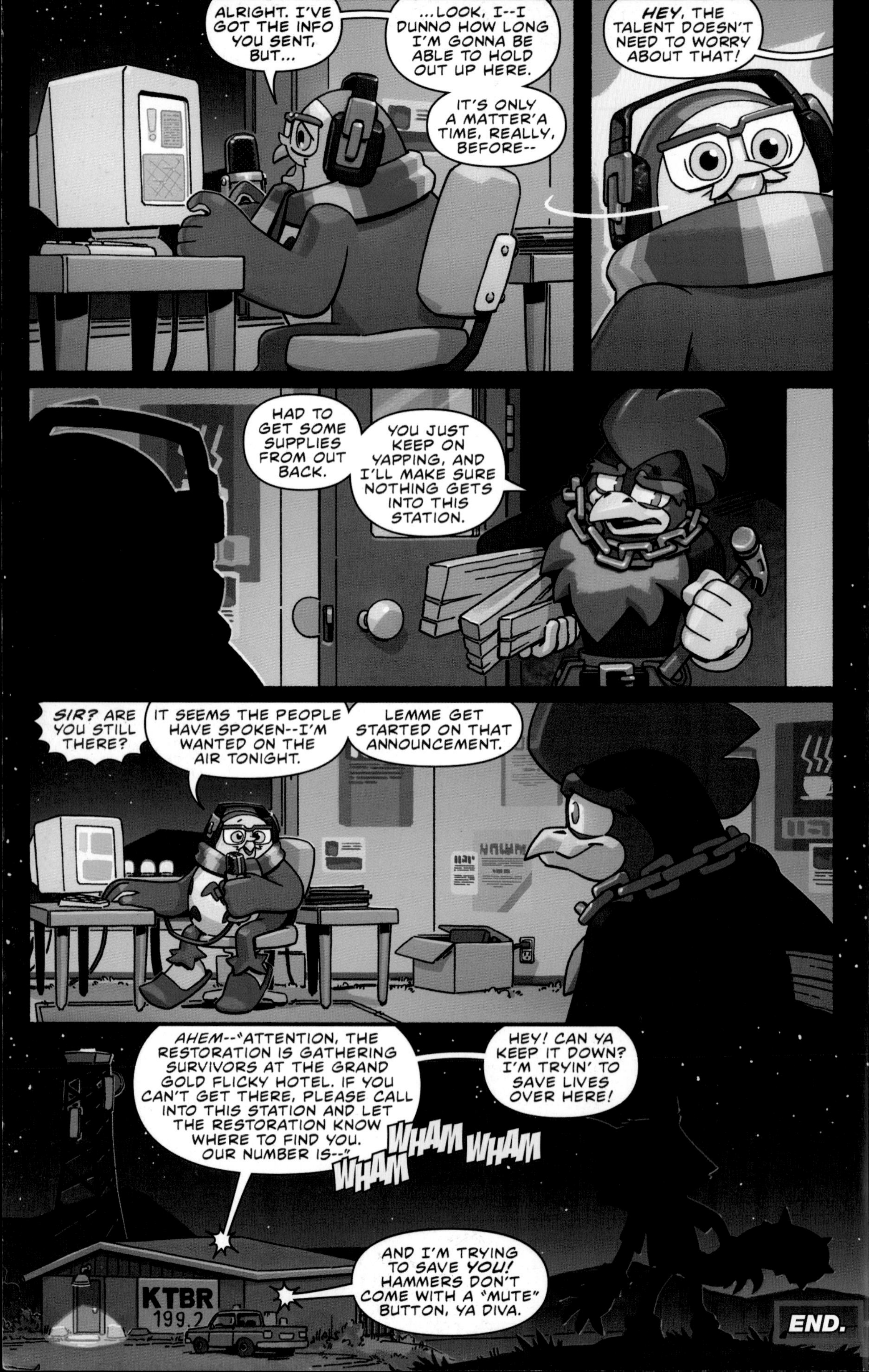

ALRIGHT. I'VE GOT THE INFO YOU SENT, BUT...
...LOOK, I--I DUNNO HOW LONG I'M GONNA BE ABLE TO HOLD OUT UP HERE.
IT'S ONLY A MATTER'A TIME, REALLY, BEFORE--
HEY, THE TALENT DOESN'T NEED TO WORRY ABOUT THAT!
HAD TO GET SOME SUPPLIES FROM OUT BACK.
YOU JUST KEEP ON YAPPING, AND I'LL MAKE SURE NOTHING GETS INTO THIS STATION.
SIR? ARE YOU STILL THERE?
IT SEEMS THE PEOPLE HAVE SPOKEN--I'M WANTED ON THE AIR TONIGHT.
LEMME GET STARTED ON THAT ANNOUNCEMENT.
AHEM--"ATTENTION, THE RESTORATION IS GATHERING SURVIVORS AT THE GRAND GOLD FLICKY HOTEL. IF YOU CAN'T GET THERE, PLEASE CALL INTO THIS STATION AND LET THE RESTORATION KNOW WHERE TO FIND YOU. OUR NUMBER IS--"
HEY! CAN YA KEEP IT DOWN? I'M TRYIN' TO SAVE LIVES OVER HERE!
WHAM WHAM WHAM
KTBR
199.2
AND I'M TRYING TO SAVE YOU! HAMMERS DON'T COME WITH A "MUTE" BUTTON, YA DIVA.
END.

METAL SONIC IN
REFLECTIONS

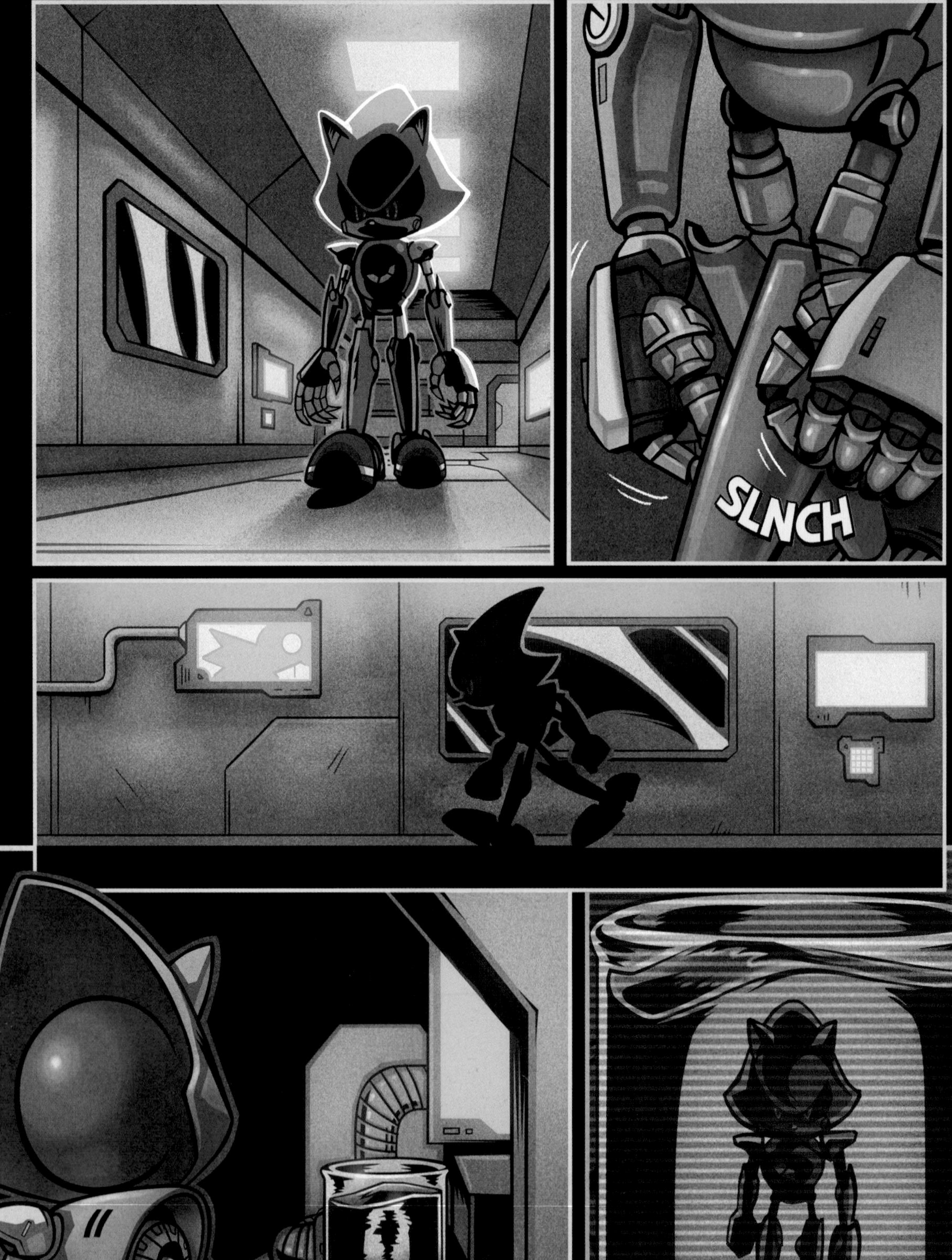
SLNCH

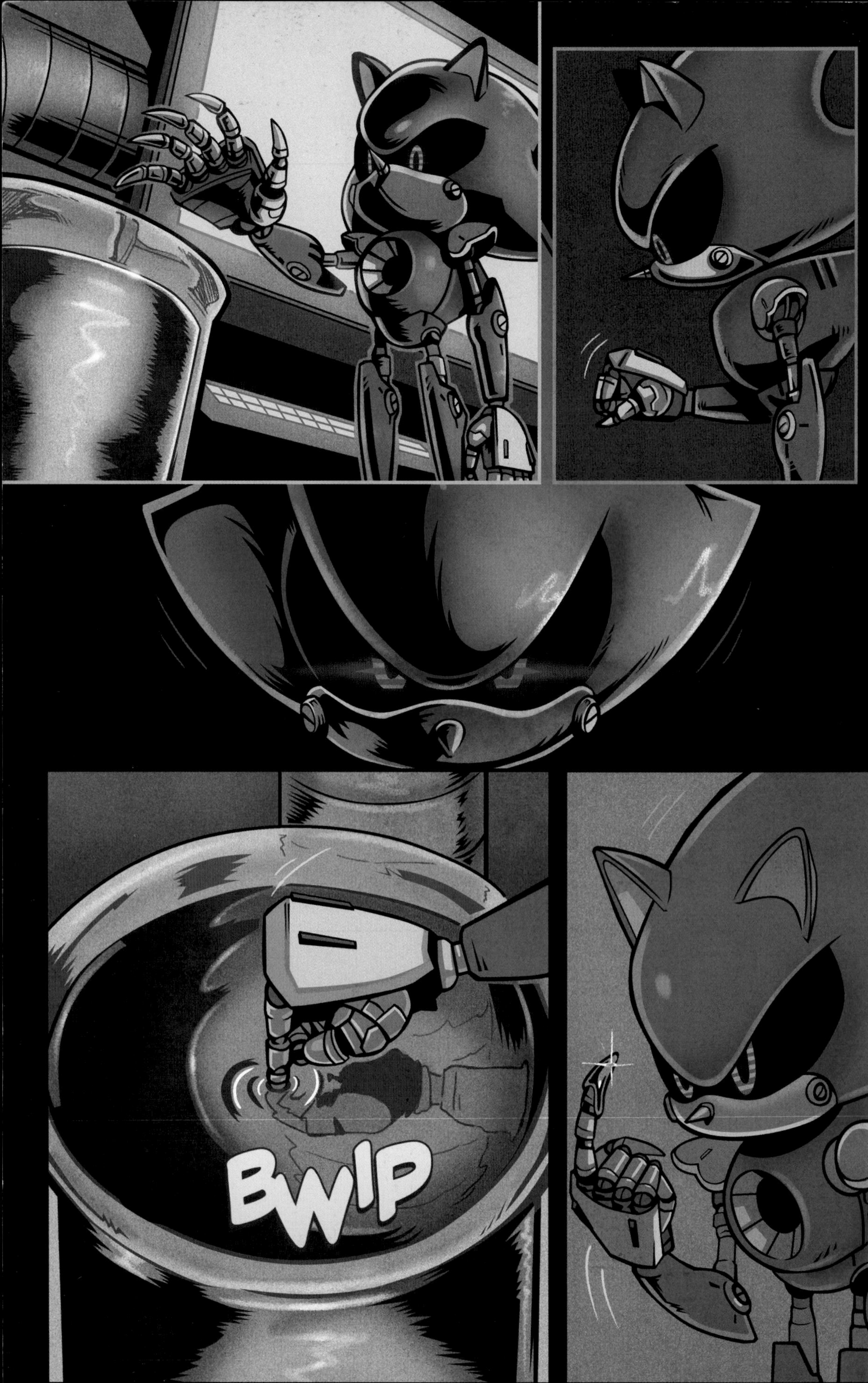
BWIP

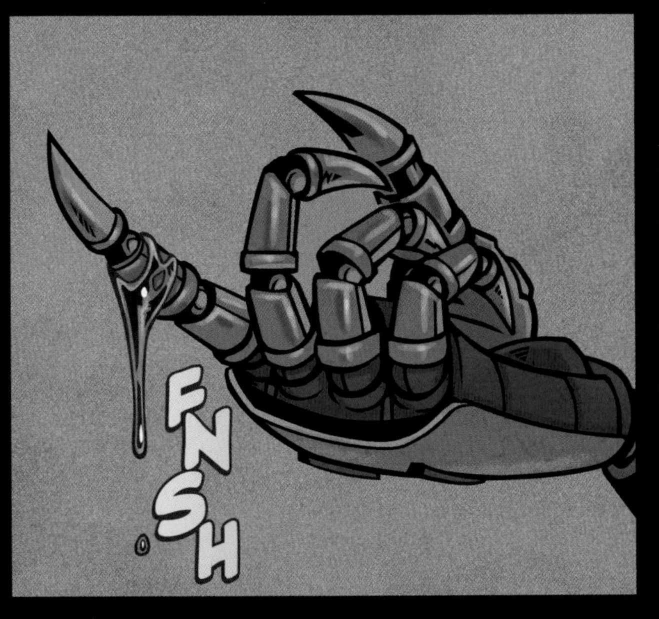
FNSH

DWOP

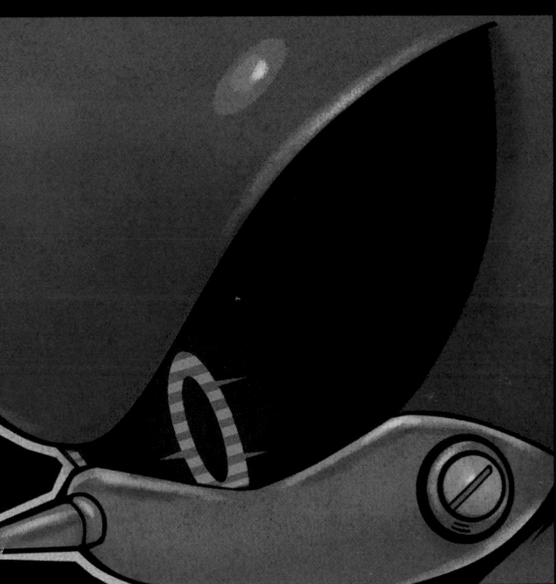

AHEM!
SNAP

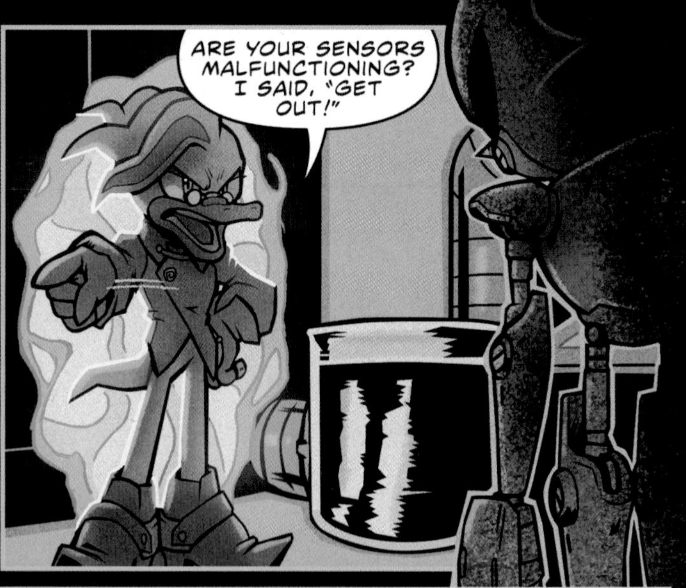
ARE YOUR SENSORS MALFUNCTIONING? I SAID, "GET OUT!"

I CAN'T BELIEVE THIS.
THE DOCTOR'S GREATEST CREATION SHAMBLING AROUND *MY* LAB LIKE A ZOMBOT.

END.

DR. STARLINE IN EGGMAN'S DAY OFF
MARVELOUS... HIS GENIUS IS COMING TO FRUITION! THE DOCTOR IS SUCH A VISIONARY!

NOW, NOW, WHAT'S THIS?

ARGH!

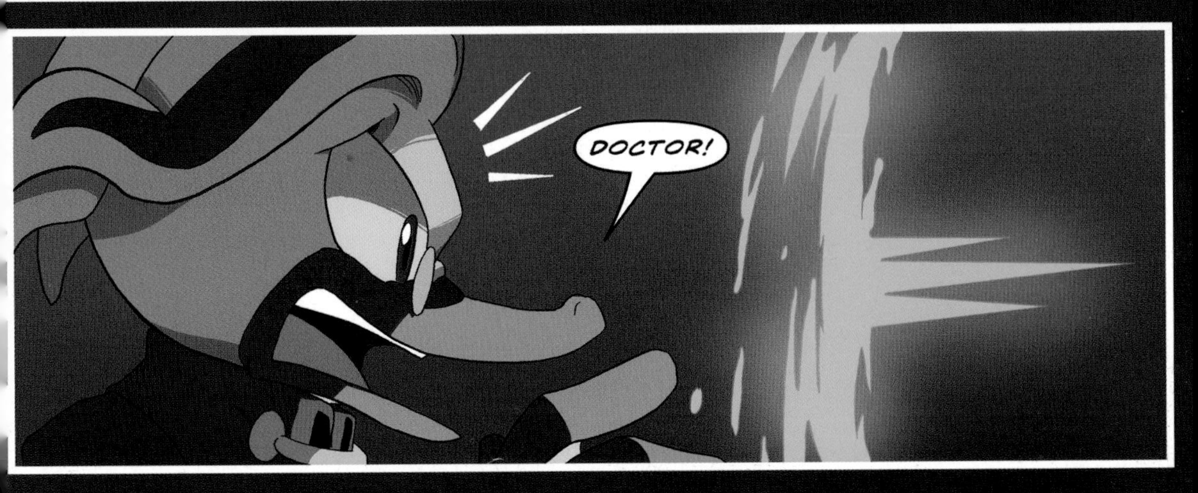
DOCTOR!

DON'T WORRY, I'M COMING, SIR!
STARLINE?!
YAAAH!
I THOUGHT YOU WERE IN TROUBLE! ARE YOU OKAY?
I WOULD BE IF I COULD FIND THE BLASTED LIGHT SWITCH!
REST ASSURED, THE ROBOT WHO INSTALLED IT AT THE BACK OF THE ROOM IS NOW SCRAP METAL.

CLICK
SINCE YOU'RE HERE, I SUPPOSE I SHOULD INTRODUCE YOU TO...

...THE EGGCAVE! HA HA HA!
MY INNER SANCTUM! MY HOME AWAY FROM HOME--BUT ACTUALLY STILL AT HOME! JUST A LITTLE MORE UNDERGROUND THAN THE OTHER ROOMS!
DO NOT TOUCH
WOW...

THIS IS WHERE I LIKE TO SPEND MY DAYS OFF AND TAKE A LITTLE TIME JUST FOR ME.
WORK ON SOME PERSONAL PROJECTS IN A QUIET SPACE WHERE I CAN FOCUS AND REALLY GET THE EGG JUICES FLOWING!

YOU KNOW, I DON'T THINK I'VE HAD ANY VISITORS HERE BEFORE.
OH! IT'S TRULY AN HONOR, SIR!

EVEN THE GREATEST MASTERMINDS NEED A HOBBY, WOULDN'T YOU AGREE?
ON MY DAYS OFF, I LIKE TO BUILD TOY ROBOTS. IT'S RELAXING, PIECING EVERYTHING TOGETHER.
BUT YOU PROMISED TO BRIEF ME THIS AFTERNOON...

AND WITH THESE TOY ROBOTS, I LIKE TO FIGURE OUT STRATEGIES AND BATTLE PLANS FOR THE WEEK AHEAD, AND, WELL...

WHAT?! THAT CURSED HEDGEHOG, FOREVER A PAIN IN MY--

BASH BASH
...PERHAPS EVIL NEVER REALLY TAKES A BREAK, DOES IT? *HA HA HA!*

--AHEM. ANYWAY. IT'S NOT ALL HEDGEHOG THIS, AND HEDGEHOG THAT--

--SOMETIMES IT'S THE FOX AND THE CHAMELEON!

SOON, MY ENEMIES WILL BECOME MY ZOMBOTS! NO MORE WILL THEY GET IN MY WAY, BUT RATHER, THEY'LL DO MY BIDDING! HA HA!

INCREDIBLE CRAFTSMANSHIP, DOCTOR!
I'M AWARE!

THESE ARE SO IMPRESSIVE, SO DETAILED, SO--

--UM.

...

IT'S MY DAY OFF, NOT YOURS! TIME FOR YOU TO LEAVE AND GET BACK TO IT!
B-B-BUT!

SLAM
WHAT HAPPENS IN THE EGGCAVE, STAYS IN THE EGGCAVE! KNOCK NEXT TIME!

EGGCAVE
END.

THE CHAOTIX IN FLOCK TOGETHER
UGH! ANOTHER DEAD END!*
*THIS STORY TAKES PLACE BEFORE STH #22–EDS.
CHARMY'S BEEN OUT THERE FOR DAYS! HE'S JUST A KID, AND HE'S ALL ALONE IN THE APOCALYPSE!
HE PROBABLY SAW THE SHIP LEAVE WITHOUT HIM AND THOUGHT WE ABANDONED HIM TO BECOME ONE OF THOSE THINGS AND...
...HOW CAN YOU BE SO CALM, ESPIO?!
WE NEED TO KEEP A LEVEL HEAD AND THINK CLEARLY.
GRR...
BLINDLY SEARCHING IS SENDING US IN CIRCLES. WE'LL HEAD BACK TO RESTORATION HQ TO DROP EVERYONE OFF, AND THEN WE CAN REFUEL AND REGROUP.
...CAN WE AT LEAST GO FASTER?!
I KNOW YOU'RE WORRIED ABOUT YOUR FRIEND, BUT WE'RE IN THE FLIGHT PATH OF A LARGE FLICKY MIGRATION. I HAVE TO FLY CAUTIOUSLY.
WE'RE DETECTIVES, VECTOR. SO IS CHARMY.
I BELIEVE IF THERE'S ANYTHING WE CAN FIND, IT'S EACH OTHER.
WHAM

YO, PILOT! WHAT'S THE SHAKE UP?!
THE... THE FLICKIES...
...THEY'RE ZOMBOTS!
WAIT...
"...CHARMY!"
YOU WERE RIGHT, ESPIO! HE FOUND US.
VECTOR, WAIT! WE NEED A PLAN!

LITTLE BUDDY! I'VE BEEN LOOKIN' EVERYWHERE FOR YOU! I PROMISE, WE DIDN'T MEAN TO LEAVE YOU BEHIND! BUT...
...BUT IT'S ALL GOOD NOW! WE'LL TAKE YOU BACK TO HQ AND GET YOU FIXED UP! TAILS IS SMART. HE'LL FIGURE SOMETHING OUT!
DON'T WORRY, CHARMY...
...I GOT... YOU?
I SAID...
...I...
...GOT...
...YOU!

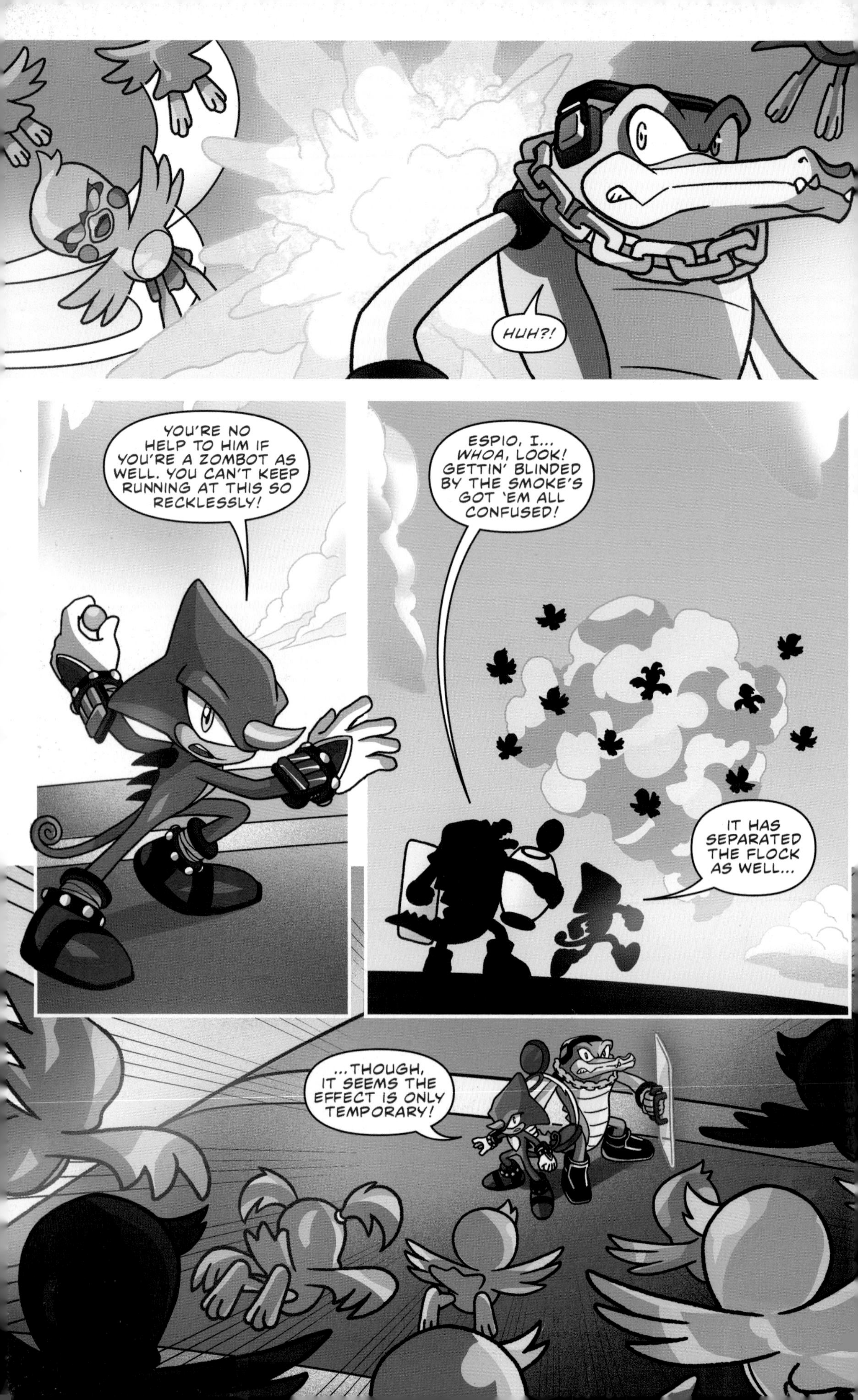
HUH?!
YOU'RE NO HELP TO HIM IF YOU'RE A ZOMBOT AS WELL. YOU CAN'T KEEP RUNNING AT THIS SO RECKLESSLY!
ESPIO, I... WHOA, LOOK! GETTIN' BLINDED BY THE SMOKE'S GOT 'EM ALL CONFUSED!
IT HAS SEPARATED THE FLOCK AS WELL...
...THOUGH, IT SEEMS THE EFFECT IS ONLY TEMPORARY!

GRR... HOW AM I SUPPOSED TO FIGURE OUT A SAFE WAY TO GET TO CHARMY WHEN I CAN'T HEAR MYSELF THINK OVER ALL THESE BIRDS AND THEIR FLAPPIN' AND BUZZIN' AND...
...BUZZIN'! ESPIO, THAT'S IT!
I HAVE A PLAN, IF YOU HAVE MY BACK.
ALWAYS.
FLAP FLAP FLAP FLAP FLAP FLAP
FLAP FLAP FLAP FLAP FLAP
FLAP BZZZZ FLAP
AHA!
FOUND YA!

GOT 'IM! LET'S JET!

HA! LOOK AT US! EVEN IN THE ZOMBOT APOCALYPSE...
...THE CHAOTIX ALWAYS FIND WHAT WE'RE LOOKIN' FOR.
END.

SPIRAL HILL VILLAGE SQUARE.
H-HAS ANYONE SEEN TANGLE? I NEED BIG HELP! I DON'T KNOW WHERE MY FRIENDS ARE! I REALLY NEED--!
OH, I KNOW YOU! YOU'RE PART OF SONIC'S FAN CLUB, YES? TANGLE TOLD ME ABOUT HOW SHE SAVED YOU FROM AN EGG PAWN!*
WHAT HAPPENED TO THE REST OF YOUR GROUP?
JEWEL THE BEETLE IN THE CATALYST
*THAT KINDA HAPPENED IN STH: ANNUAL 2019-EDS.

OUR CLUB WAS MEETING WAAAY OUT IN THE FARMS! BUT... THEN A BIG SHIP STARTED DROPPING WEIRD GUNK FROM THE SKY. EVERYONE WAS RUNNIN'! AND THEN I-I GOT SEPARATED AND...
...IT'S BEEN ALMOST AN HOUR AND I-I'M SCARED! I'M THEIR PRESIDENT! IT'S MY DUTY TO FIND MY FRIENDS IF THEY'RE MISSING! I-I'M...
SNIFF

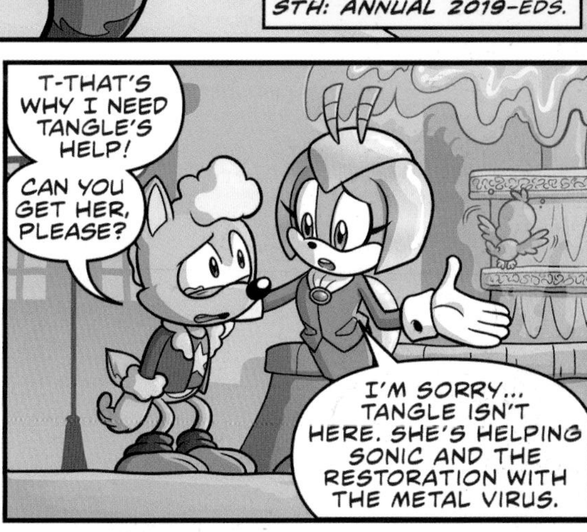

T-THAT'S WHY I NEED TANGLE'S HELP!
CAN YOU GET HER, PLEASE?
I'M SORRY... TANGLE ISN'T HERE. SHE'S HELPING SONIC AND THE RESTORATION WITH THE METAL VIRUS.

OH.
BUT...

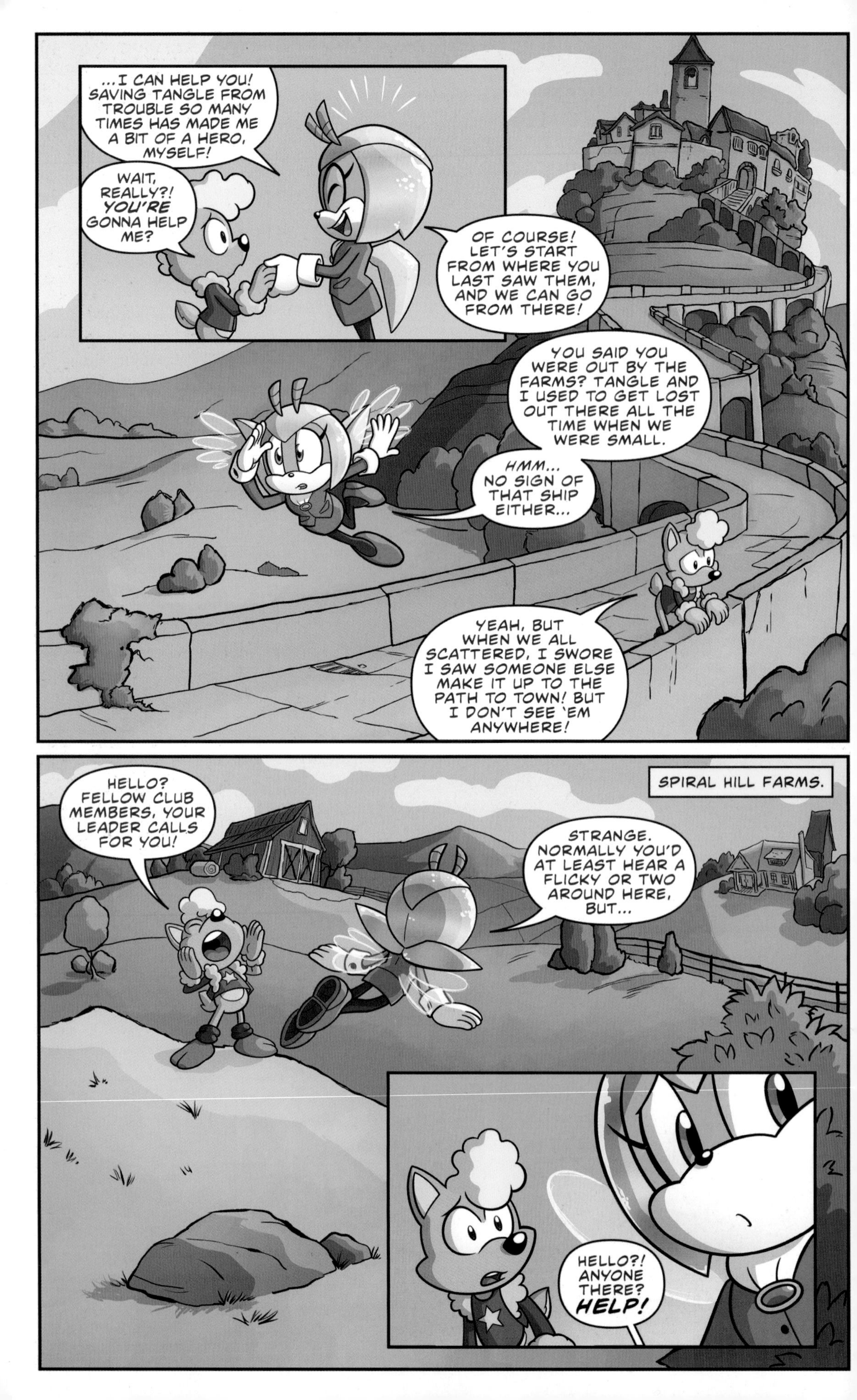
...I CAN HELP YOU! SAVING TANGLE FROM TROUBLE SO MANY TIMES HAS MADE ME A BIT OF A HERO, MYSELF!
WAIT, REALLY?! YOU'RE GONNA HELP ME?
OF COURSE! LET'S START FROM WHERE YOU LAST SAW THEM, AND WE CAN GO FROM THERE!
YOU SAID YOU WERE OUT BY THE FARMS? TANGLE AND I USED TO GET LOST OUT THERE ALL THE TIME WHEN WE WERE SMALL.
HMM... NO SIGN OF THAT SHIP EITHER...
YEAH, BUT WHEN WE ALL SCATTERED, I SWORE I SAW SOMEONE ELSE MAKE IT UP TO THE PATH TO TOWN! BUT I DON'T SEE 'EM ANYWHERE!
SPIRAL HILL FARMS.
HELLO? FELLOW CLUB MEMBERS, YOUR LEADER CALLS FOR YOU!
STRANGE. NORMALLY YOU'D AT LEAST HEAR A FLICKY OR TWO AROUND HERE, BUT...
HELLO?! ANYONE THERE? HELP!

IT'S COMING FROM THIS WAY!

VICE PRES! WE'RE HERE TO--
GASP
OH, NO.

GNGH-- ABOUT TIME SOMEONE FOUND ME!
WHAT'RE YOU DOIN' STANDIN' AROUND FOR? HELP!

JEWEL... WHAT'S UP WITH THIS SHINY STUFF, ANYWAY?
DON'T TOUCH IT. TANGLE TOLD ME ABOUT THIS... IT'S NOT SAFE.
STAY HERE, I'M GOING TO HELP HER.

HI THERE, I'M JEWEL. ARE YOU OKAY? WHAT HAPPENED?
UGH... THERE WAS THIS BIG, DUMB SHIP SPEWING OUT THAT WEIRD STUFF, SO I RAN AND HID HERE. NOT T-THAT I WAS SCARED OR ANYTHING!

WELL, THANK GOODNESS NONE OF IT'S ON YOU.
WHY? WHAT'S WRONG WITH IT...?

IT'D BE VERY BAD. SONIC IS... TRYING TO STOP IT. TANGLE TOO. BUT IT'S VERY DANGEROUS.
NOW THEN, WE SHOULD HEAD BACK HOME.
Y-YEAH! THAT'S A GOOD...

...IDEA?

SWWOOSH
EEEK!

ARE THOSE... OUR FRIENDS? HEY GUYS! GUYS!
ZOMBOTS! DON'T DRAW THEIR ATTENTION. WE NEED TO HURRY, BEFORE THEY SEE US!
ZOMB-WHAT? THOSE'RE MY CONSTI-TUENTS!
DON'CHA MEAN MY CONSTITIENTS? I WON THE RACE Y'KNOW!

THEY'RE EVERYWHERE!
IS IT ME OR IS THAT SHIP FROM BEFORE COMING CLOSER?!
DON'T GET DISTRACTED! COME ON, WE'RE ALMOST THERE!
BUT WHAT ARE THEY?!

YES! SAFE AND SOUND. NOW, ARE YOUR HOMES--?
HA! WE DID IT! WE MADE IT!

OH...

...YOU BOTH TOUCHED THAT?
UM...
I MEAN, I HAD SOME OF THAT STUFF ON ME, BUT I FEEL FINE...
THIS IS SOMETHING WE CAN WASH OFF... RIGHT?

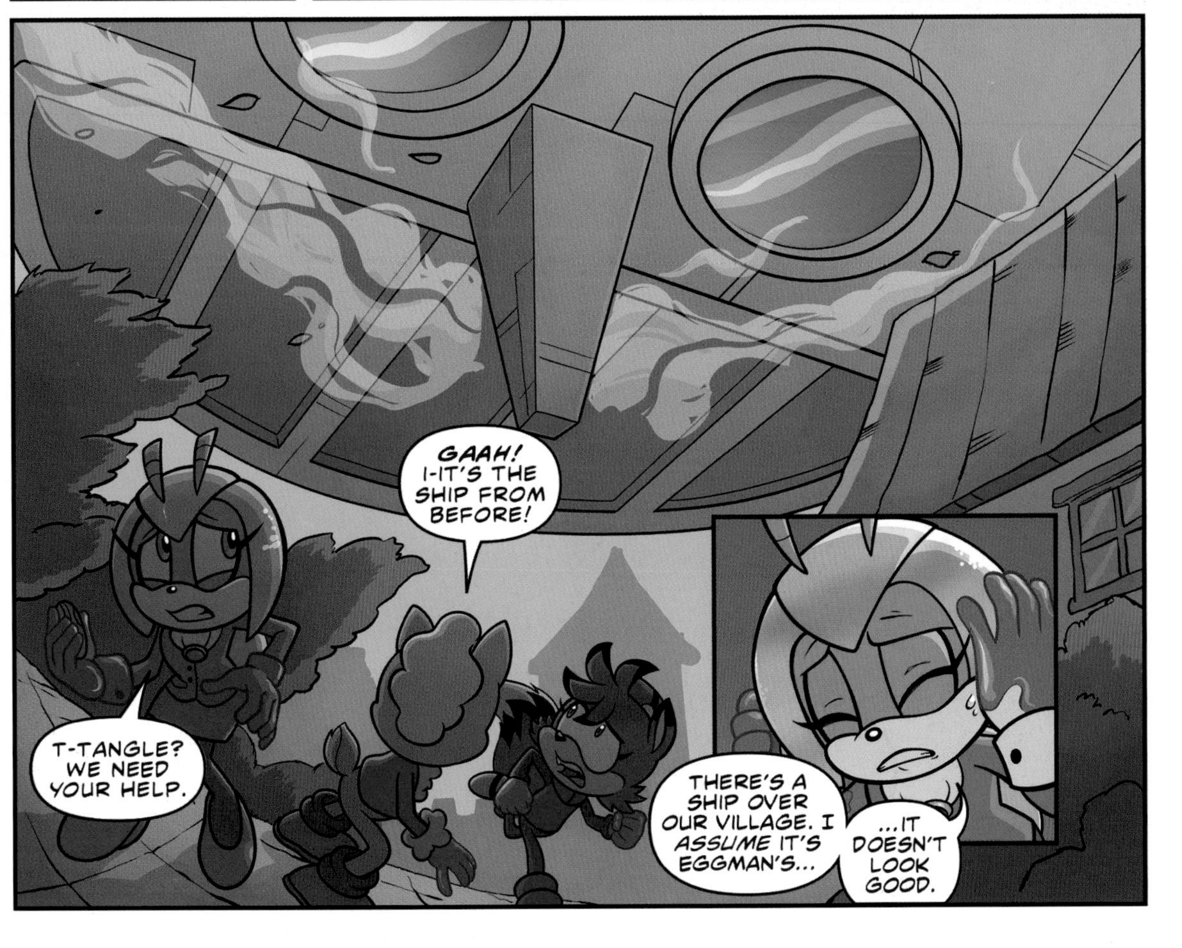
GAAH! I-IT'S THE SHIP FROM BEFORE!
T-TANGLE? WE NEED YOUR HELP.
THERE'S A SHIP OVER OUR VILLAGE. I ASSUME IT'S EGGMAN'S...
...IT DOESN'T LOOK GOOD.

JEWEL? YOU HERE?
LATER...

CREEEK

I CAME AS FAST AS I COULD! ARE YOU OKAY? ARE YOU...

...S-STILL YOU?
END.

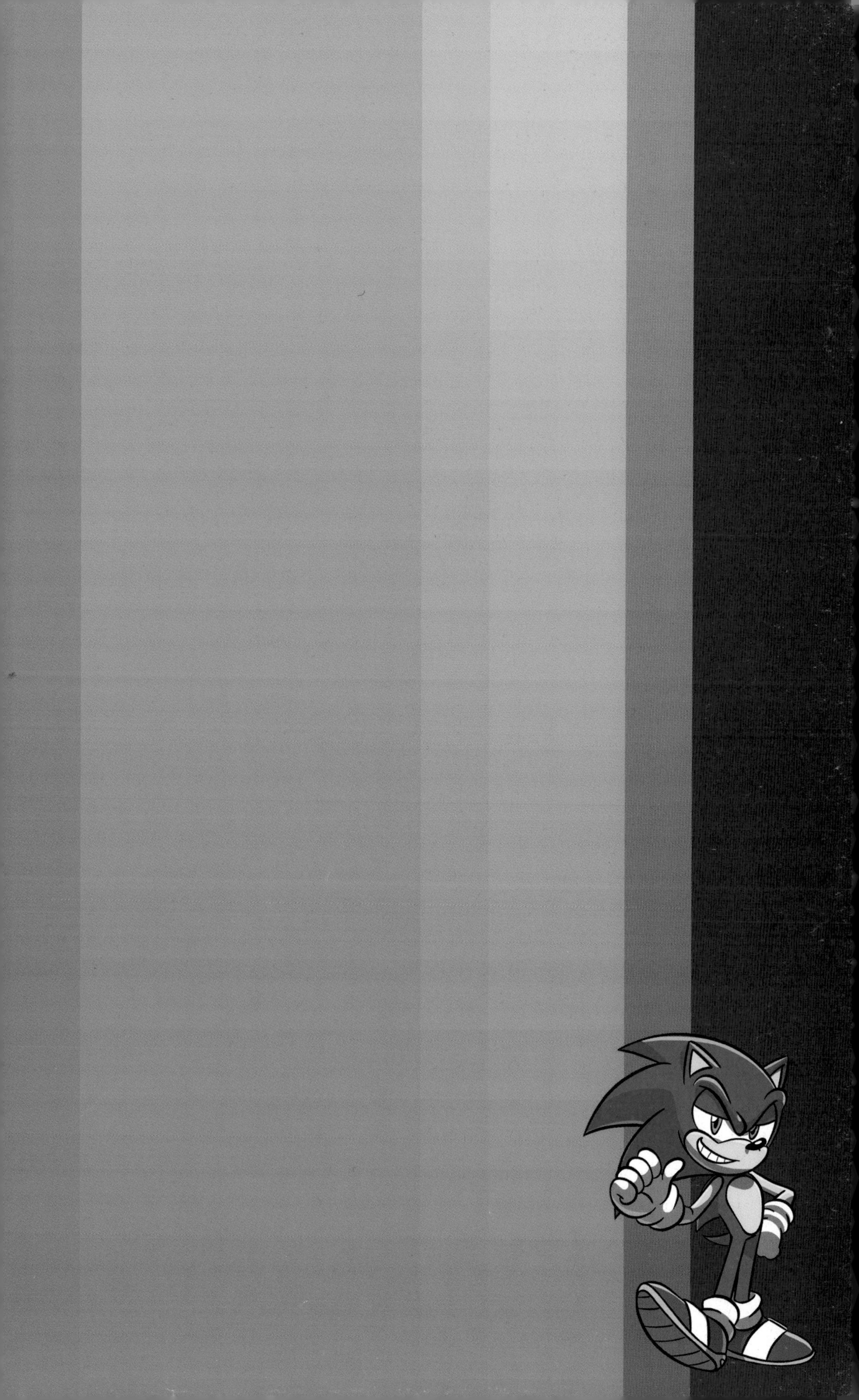

ART BY **ADAM BRYCE THOMAS**

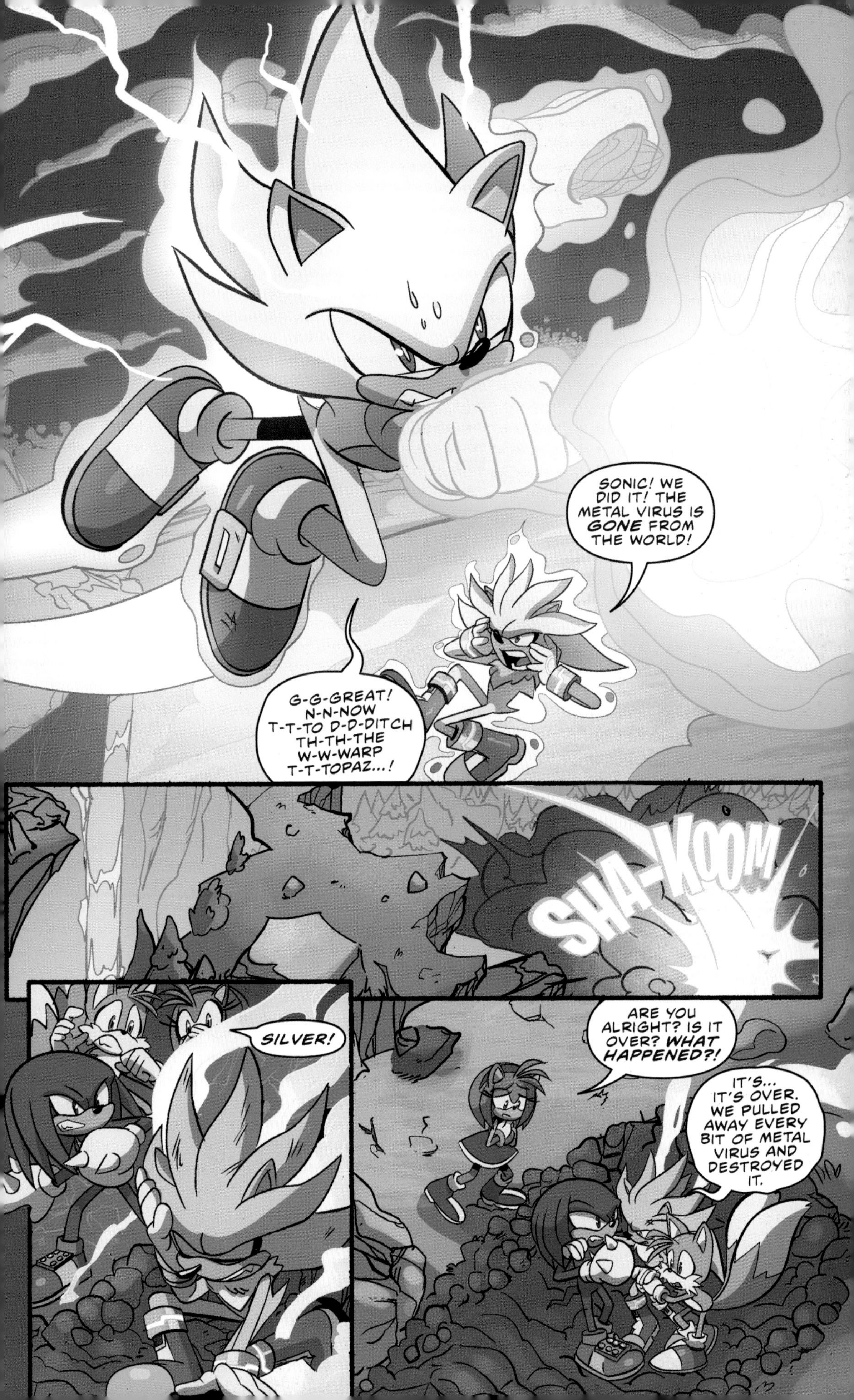
SONIC! WE DID IT! THE METAL VIRUS IS GONE FROM THE WORLD!
G-G-GREAT! N-N-NOW T-T-TO D-D-DITCH TH-TH-THE W-W-WARP T-T-TOPAZ...!
SHA-KOOM
SILVER!
ARE YOU ALRIGHT? IS IT OVER? WHAT HAPPENED?!
IT'S... IT'S OVER. WE PULLED AWAY EVERY BIT OF METAL VIRUS AND DESTROYED IT.

BUT... DR. STARLINE WAS RIGHT. THE WARP TOPAZ COULDN'T HANDLE ALL THAT POWER.
SONIC TRIED TO DITCH IT IN THE SUPER WARP PORTAL, BUT...
...OH, NO.

TCH! HE'S JUST BEING DRAMATIC. HE'LL COME FLOATING DOWN, ALL GOLDEN AND SMUG, ANY MINUTE NOW.

AAAANY MINUTE NOW.
IS THERE A WAY WE COULD... I DON'T KNOW, ***SEARCH*** FOR HIM?
HE WAS AT THE CENTER OF CHAOS EMERALD-FUELED WARP TOPAZ DISTORTIONS. I WOULDN'T KNOW WHERE TO BEGIN.

"DARN IT, SONIC! YOU'RE MAKING ME LOOK BAD! KNOCK IT OFF AND COME BACK!"
"OH, ***BOO-HOO!*** OUR HERO MADE THE ULTIMATE SACRIFICE!"
PLEASE. IT'S LIKE I'M THE ONLY ONE WHO ***REALLY*** KNOWS THAT INSUFFERABLE BLUE NUISANCE.
STILL, WHILE THEY'RE ALL BUSY WRINGING THEIR HANDS OVER SONIC, I'LL MAKE MY TACTICAL RETREAT.
GOOD THING I TOOK SPECIAL CARE TO REPURPOSE ONLY ***NON-ESSENTIAL*** PARTS OF THE SHUTTLE FOR THAT PORTAL DEVICE!

MOTHER... I DIDN'T SEE MR. SONIC RETURN TO ANGEL ISLAND.
WELL... IT WAS A VERY BRIGHT FLASH. PERHAPS WE JUST MISSED HIM?
GEMERL, I KNOW YOU'VE HAD A VERY BUSY DAY, BUT WOULD YOU MIND LOOKING FOR... GEMERL? WHAT'S WRONG?
OH, NO! MOTHER-- LOOK OUT! IT'S--!
ME.
STOP IT! ALL YOUR MEAN FRIENDS WERE BEATEN! THE BAD TIMES ARE OVER! JUST GO HOME!
NO.

I WILL NOT SUFFER HUMILIATION FROM SONIC *AGAIN!* I WILL NEVER ACCEPT DEFEAT!
I HAVE LOST THE METAL VIRUS AND THE ZOMBOT HORDE.
I HAVE LOST THE POWER OF THE CHAOS EMERALD...
...SO I WILL TEAR THIS WORLD ASUNDER WITH MY *BARE HANDS!*
NO! MR. SONIC WILL COME BACK AND STOP YOU!
THEN YOU WON'T BE HERE TO WELCOME HIS RETURN! ANY LAST WORDS, WHELP?
YES, SIR.
CHEESE! GET 'IM!
POW

YOU DARE?!
SOK
YEAH, WE DO!
ALRIGHT, BOYS...
...LET'S TAKE HIM DOWN!
RAAUGH

I.
WILL.
NOT.
FALL!
CLUD
THEN YOU'LL BE CRUSHED!
I... WILL... HAVE... MY... REVENGE... ON... YOU... ALL...

WHEW THE FINAL CRISIS AVERTED...
YOU SAY THAT, BUT...
ANY!
SECOND!
NOW!

TAILS... PLEASE. WE JUST PREVENTED THE END OF THE WORLD AND SONIC MAY BE LOST TO US. I DON'T KNOW HOW MUCH MORE I CAN TAKE.
ME TOO. BUT ZAVOK WAS JUST ONE OF THE DEADLY SIX. THE OTHER FIVE ARE STILL OUT THERE.

RIVERSIDE.
"AND THAT'S A VERY BIG PROBLEM."
THAT'S RIGHT! YOU BETTER RUN!
AW, MAN... AFTER I CRUSH THESE FOOLS, THEN WHAT? WHAT DO I TEAR UP NEXT? WHERE DO I GO?
ARGH! I'VE NEVER HAD TO THINK THIS MUCH BEFORE! IT'S KILLIN' MY KILLER MOOD!
LET'S GO FIND ZAVOK! HE'LL TELL US WHAT TO DO!

SUNSET CITY.
I SAID "BACK OFF!"
IT'S BAD ENOUGH YOU INGRATES WON'T DO WHAT I SAY! NOW YOU'RE MAKING ME DO MY OWN FIGHTING?!
WELL IF ZAVOK'S PLAN FAILED, THEN I'M OUT...
...BUT I WON'T FORGET THIS.
YOU'RE ALL GOING TO SUFFER FOR THIS INDIGNITY.
ORCHARDVILLE.
ANY SIGN OF THE WEIRDO WHO WAS CONTROLLING US?
NO. AND GLEN HASN'T COME BACK.
OH, MAN... STICK CLOSE TO ME, OKAY?
HEE-HEE! YOUR FRIEND WON'T BE MOVING ANY TIME SOON!
I REALLY SHOULDN'T BE ENJOYING MYSELF LIKE THIS BUT...
...DESPERATE AND ALL ALONE? SURROUNDED BY FEAR AND HATRED? SLINKING BETWEEN THE SHADOWS?
THIS IS ALMOST AS GOOD AS TERRORIZING THE WORLD WITH ZOMBOTS!

VISTA VIEW.
BRING MORE STUFF TO WEIGH THIS DOWN! HURRY! WE'VE GOT TO KEEP IT TRAPPED!
NNNNGH...
AWW... I LOOK LIKE A WAFFLE...
HEY, WAIT!
BRING ME WAFFLES!
WINTERBURG.
BUFFOONS. THE INSTANT THEY THINK THE THREAT IS OVER, THEY START CELEBRATING.
SUCH JUBILATION WILL BE THEIR DOWNFALL. BUT FIRST--I MUST FIND ZAVOK AND DEVISE OUR COUNTER-OFFENSIVE.
AND WHILE IT PAINS ME TO ADMIT IT...

"...THE BABYLON ROGUES HAVE EARNED THEIR VICTORY."
WE'RE ALIVE! WE'RE OKAY! WE'RE NOT ZOMBOTS!
YEAH-YEAH-YEAH! PUT ME DOWN, YA BIG PALOOKA!
JET? ARE YOU OKAY?
YOU'RE WASTING A WORRY. I'M FINE.
THAT WAS CLOSE. TOO CLOSE. WHERE'S THAT SHRIVELED OLD MAN? I WANT TO TURN THAT PRUNE INTO JUICE!

IF HE KNOWS WHAT'S GOOD FOR HIM, HE'S ALREADY ON THE RUN.
YEAH. BUT YOU KNOW WHO DIDN'T RUN? YOU. YOU STUCK WITH US TO THE BITTER END. THAT WAS INCREDIBLY BRAVE AND NOBLE OF YOU, JET.
R-REALLY...?

I MEAN--YEAH, DUH, OF COURSE I STUCK AROUND! I'M THE LEGENDARY WIND MASTER! THE BRAVEST, NOBLEST, BESTEST LEADER OF ALL TIME!
AAAAND THE MOMENT IS RUINED.
YOU SURE ARE, BOSS! YOU SURE ARE!

UGH... SO I GUESS ONCE I GET BACK TO RESTORATION HQ--*IF* IT'S STILL STANDING--I'VE GOT TO WORRY ABOUT *THEM* NOW.
M-MAYBE YOU SHOULD TAKE A BREAK FROM THAT? WHY DID YOU EVEN TAKE ON THAT JOB TO BEGIN WITH?
BECAUSE *SOMEBODY* DISSOLVED THE RESISTANCE ON A WHIM!*
THE WAR WAS OVER. MY PLACE IS UP HERE. YOU COULD'VE SAID "NO."
AND LEFT ALL THOSE PEOPLE TO REBUILD WITHOUT HELP?!
*STH#12
THERE YOU GO AGAIN, TRYING TO HELP EVERYONE EVERYWHERE.
SPEAKING OF WHICH--ZOMBOT APOCALYPSE IS OVER. WHEN ARE YOU GETTING THE REFUGEES OFF MY ISLAND?
AS SOON AS I REPAIR THE SHUTTLE WE USED FOR PARTS... WAIT...
WHERE'S THE SHUTTLE?!
UP THERE.
WHO'S FLYING THE--*WAIT!*
HOW DID WE FORGET ABOUT EGGMAN?!
IT'S JUST ONE HEADACHE AFTER ANOTHER WITH YOU PEOPLE. SPEAKING OF WHICH...

...EGGMAN ESCAPED. WEREN'T YOU SUPPOSED TO BE WATCHING HIM?
YOU'RE THE GUARDIAN OF THIS PLACE. SHOULDN'T *YOU*?
NOT MY PROBLEM ANYMORE. YOUR TIME'S UP. SCRAM.
AWW... JUST FIVE MORE MINUTES?

I TOLERATED YOU *THIS* LONG SINCE YOU HELPED SAVE THE WORLD.
DON'T MAKE ME *THROW* YOU OFF THE ISLAND.

YOU'RE SO STUBBORN. UNTIL NEXT TIME, HANDSOME.

ANY MINUTE NOW.

EGGNET SIGNAL DETECTED. SEARCHING FOR SOURCE.
SOURCE LOCATED.
UM... BOSS? WE'VE BEEN DISCOVERED.
RETRIEVAL IS ON THE WAY!
ALERT! ALERRR--
SHUNK
GEMERL!
WHERE WAS HE HIDING?!

SKYOW
BWOOOMH
I'LL GET HIM! LEMME AT HIM!
WE ARE NOT DOING THAT AGAIN! SILVER! GRAB HIM!
I'VE GOT MY HANDS FULL! SHADOW! CAN YOU--!
--OH.

GOOD TO SEE YOU AGAIN AND IN GOOD HEALTH, BOSS.
NO NEED TO SUCK UP TO ME, CUBOT. CRASHING THE FACESHIP WAS A NECESSARY EVIL.

AH, BUT WE ALREADY FOUND YOU A CONSOLATION PRIZE. OMEGA'S HEAD!
DESTROY ALL EGGMAN ROBOTS! RED DRONE! USE ME TO BLUDGEON THE YELLOW DRONE, THEN YOURSELF!
WHY DO I HAVE TO HOLD HIM?!

OOOH! THE WAYWARD FINAL MODEL IN MY E-100 LINE! WHAT A DELIGHTFUL SURPRISE! I KNOW JUST HOW TO USE YOU TO CRUSH SONIC'S LITTLE FRIENDS!
NO REST FOR THE WICKED, EH, BOSS?

BREEP BREEP
SONIC IS M.I.A. I NEED TO STRIKE WHILE THE IRON IS HOT.

SHADOW IS CLOSING IN ON US! METAL SONIC! SLOW HIM DOWN SO I CAN REACH A SECURE ESCAPE ALTITUDE!

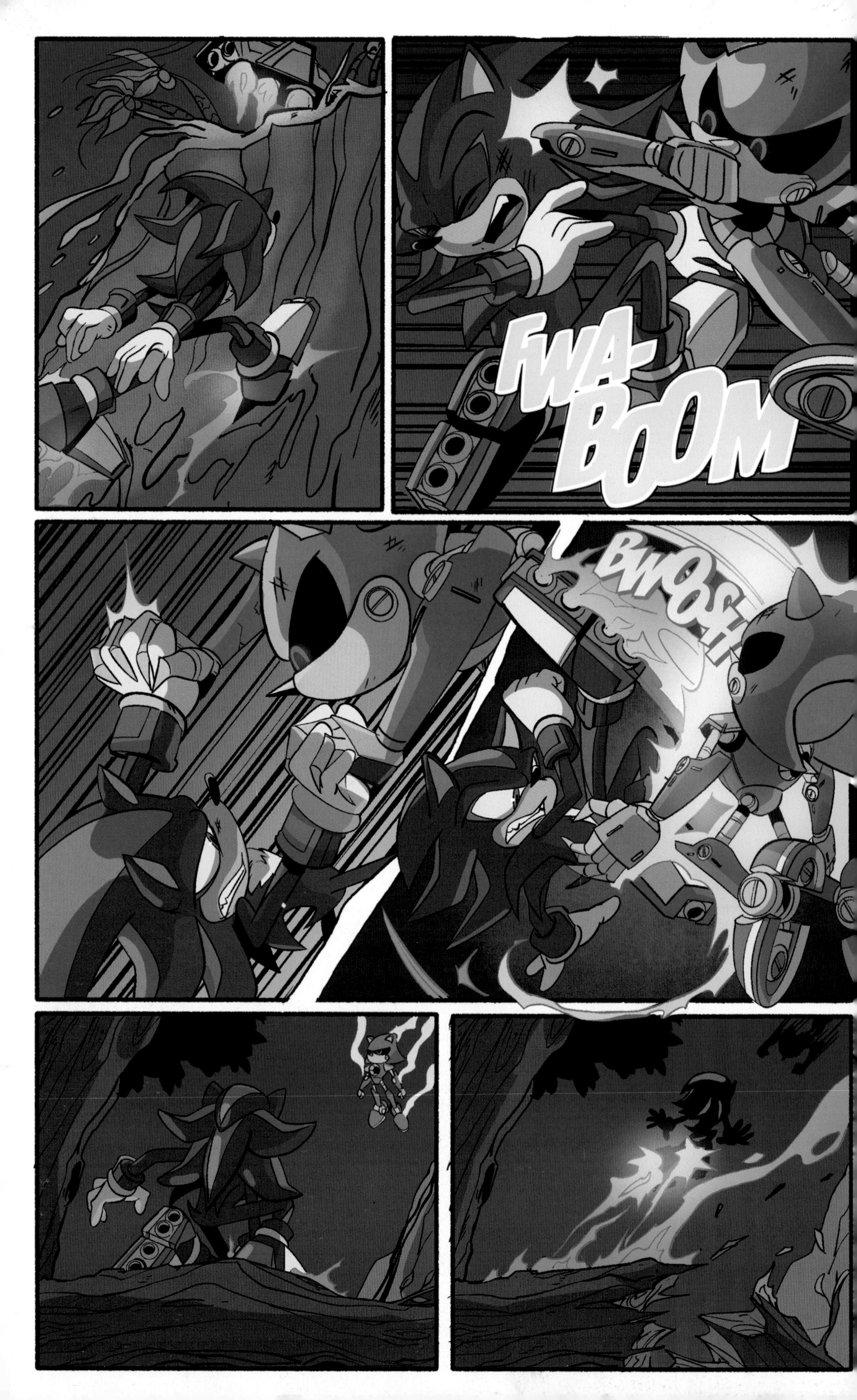
FWA-
BOOM
BWOOSH!

POW
WHAM
WHAM
KZZT

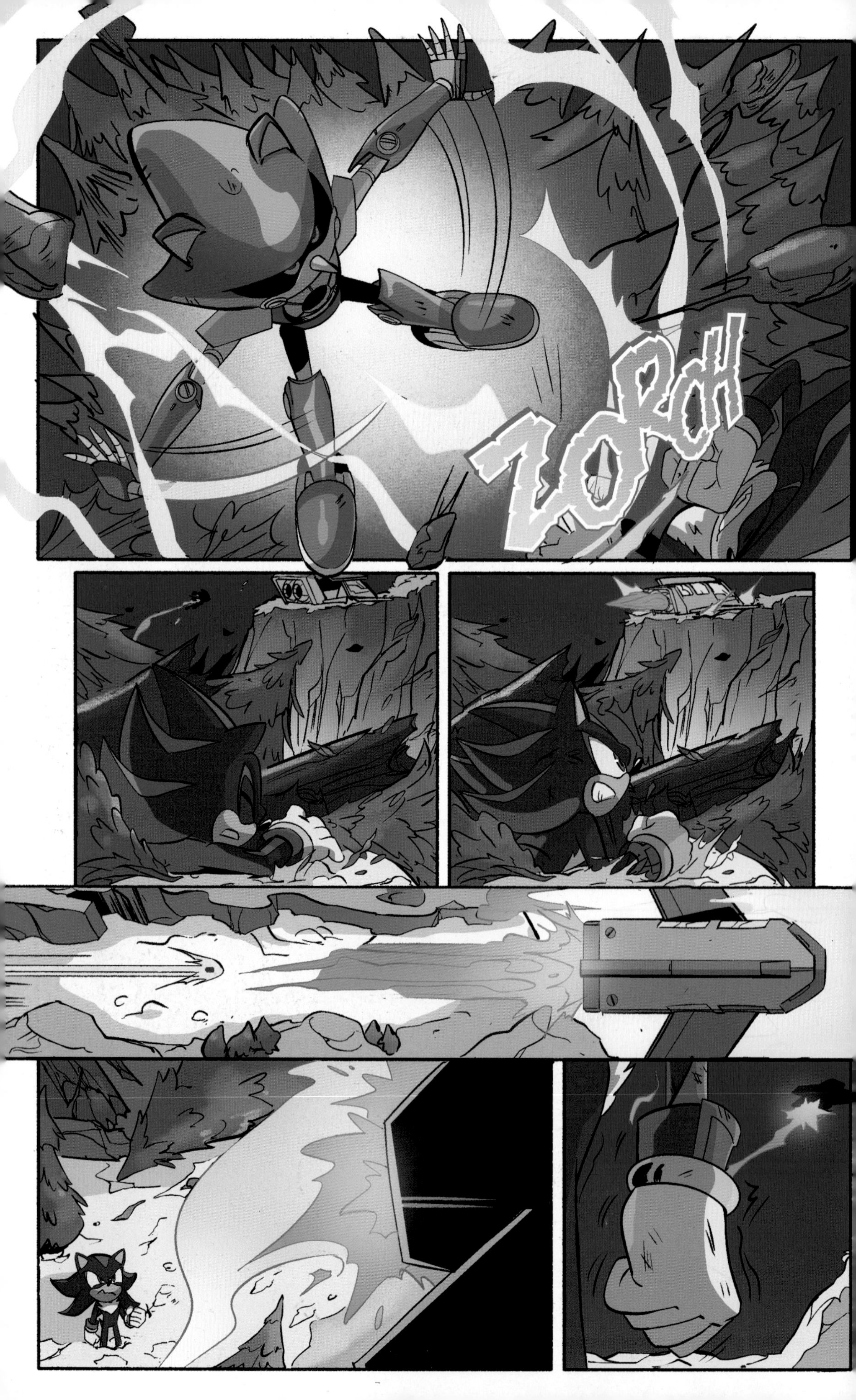
ZORCH

MEANWHILE...
THE IMPERIAL PALACE OF THE SOL EMPIRE. BLAZE'S WORLD & DIMENSION.

I COME WITH THE EVENING SECURITY REPORT, YOUR HIGHNESS.
PROCEED, GARDON.

THERE IS NOTHING TO REPORT. ALL IS PEACEFUL.

AND MAY THAT BE YOUR REPORT FOR MANY NIGHTS TO COME.

SHA-BOOM

W-WAIT, PRINCESS! IT COULD BE DANGEROUS!
IF IT THREATENS ME IN MY OWN HOME, I WILL SHOW IT WHO IS "DANGEROUS."
IS... IS THAT...?!
YES!
IT'S SONIC THE HEDGEHOG!

ART BY **JONATHAN GRAY** COLORS BY **REGGIE GRAHAM**

IMPERIAL PALACE OF THE SOL EMPIRE.
BLAZE THE CAT'S WORLD AND DIMENSION.
THE SONIC THE HEDGEHOG I KNOW WAS A HERO, A PARAGON.
HE WAS AS SWIFT AND FREE AS THE WIND. HE HAD NO MASTER, BUT FOUGHT FOR ANYONE AND EVERYONE.
THERE WAS NO CHALLENGE TOO GREAT, NO THREAT TOO DIRE THAT HE WOULDN'T FACE WITHOUT SWAGGER AND A SMILE.
HE SOUNDS VERY IMPRESSIVE. I'D LIKE TO MEET HIM ONE DAY.

I... WHO DO YOU THINK YOU ARE?
I'M AFRAID I HAVEN'T THE FOGGIEST, YOUR HIGHNESS.
I MET THE MOST PRECOCIOUS LITTLE GIRL, THOUGH, WHO DUBBED ME "MR. NEEDLEMOUSE."
I LIKE THE SOUND OF THAT.
YOU'VE HAD SOME TIME TO REST AND THINK. DO YOU RECALL ANYTHING?
NOTHING CONCRETE. ALL MY MEMORIES SEEM... WARPED.
I DREAM OF SEA AND SKY. OF GOLDEN FIRE AND A SENSE OF... FALLING.
AND THAT'S ALL!
WHAT IN THE WORLD DID THIS TO YOU, SONIC?

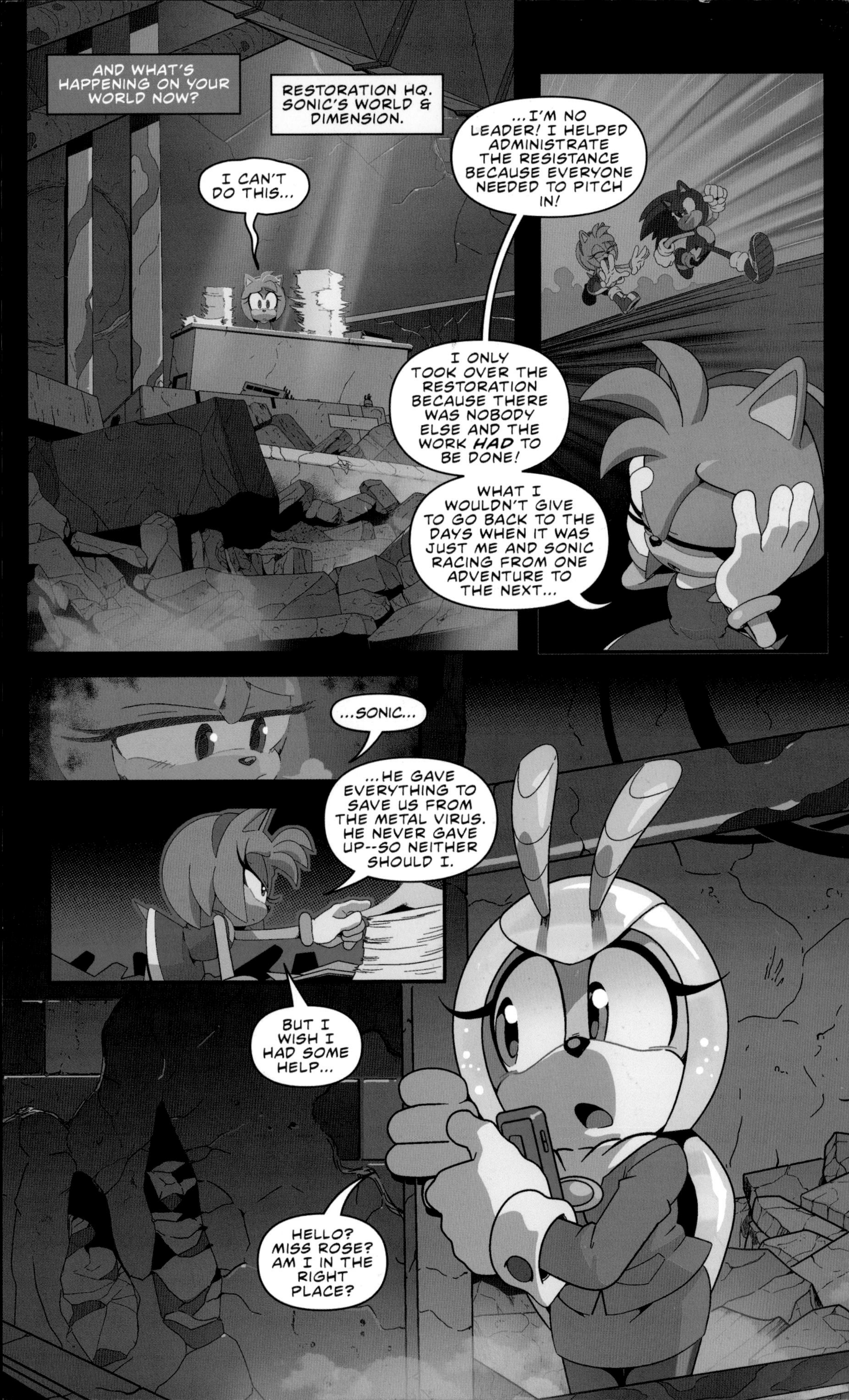
AND WHAT'S HAPPENING ON YOUR WORLD NOW?
RESTORATION HQ. SONIC'S WORLD & DIMENSION.
I CAN'T DO THIS...
...I'M NO LEADER! I HELPED ADMINISTRATE THE RESISTANCE BECAUSE EVERYONE NEEDED TO PITCH IN!
I ONLY TOOK OVER THE RESTORATION BECAUSE THERE WAS NOBODY ELSE AND THE WORK HAD TO BE DONE!
WHAT I WOULDN'T GIVE TO GO BACK TO THE DAYS WHEN IT WAS JUST ME AND SONIC RACING FROM ONE ADVENTURE TO THE NEXT...
...SONIC...
...HE GAVE EVERYTHING TO SAVE US FROM THE METAL VIRUS. HE NEVER GAVE UP--SO NEITHER SHOULD I.
BUT I WISH I HAD SOME HELP...
HELLO? MISS ROSE? AM I IN THE RIGHT PLACE?

PLEASE, CALL ME AMY. AND YOU ARE?
JEWEL, CURATOR OF SPIRAL HILL'S MINERAL MUSEUM. I'M A FRIEND OF TANGLE'S.
AH-- OKAY! SHE'S MENTIONED YOU. WHAT CAN I DO FOR YOU?
THE OTHER WAY AROUND, ACTUALLY. SHE TOLD ME HOW YOU WEREN'T ENJOYING THE RIGORS OF RUNNING THINGS--AND THAT WAS BEFORE THE PLAGUE.
I ENJOY CATALOGING AND ORGANIZING. I SEE THIS ROOM AND FEEL EXCITED AT THE IDEA OF BRINGING IT ALL TO ORDER.
SO IF YOU LIKE, I'M OFFERING TO TAKE OVER ADMINISTRATION OF THE RESTORATION AND GIVE YOU A BREAK.
THANK YOU.
O-OH MY. I DIDN'T REALIZE YOU WERE SO... STRAINED.
YOU'RE A LIFE-SAVER, JEWEL!
BUT UNLIKE A CERTAIN ECHIDNA I KNOW, I'LL MAKE SURE YOU'RE UP TO SPEED BEFORE STEPPING DOWN.
I'D APPRECIATE THAT. WHAT ARE OUR PRIMARY GOALS?
ORGANIZING SUPPLIES FOR REBUILDING...

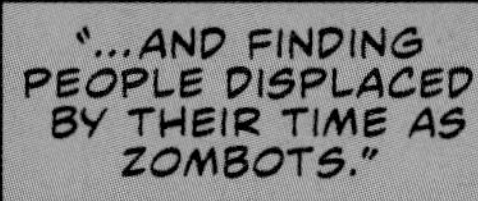
"...AND FINDING PEOPLE DISPLACED BY THEIR TIME AS ZOMBOTS."

PAFF
GAH! CAVE SPIDER!

ECHO MINE.

NO WAY OUT.
BELLIES STARTING TO GRUMBLE.
LOOKS LIKE THIS IS THE END FOR ROUGH &TUMBLE!

YOU GUYS OKAY?

GRAB MY TAIL! I'LL HELP HAUL YOU OUT!

WOO-HOO! WE'RE SAVED!
IT JUST AIN'T FAIR...

AND TO ADD INSULT TO INJURY...
WHAT'S THE DEAL? HOW COME YOU'RE BEING NICE TO US?
SONIC CURED THE WORLD OF THE METAL VIRUS--THE GUNK EGGMAN TRICKED YOU TWO INTO USING.
HE GAVE THE WHOLE WORLD A SECOND CHANCE, SO WE'RE MAKING SURE EVERYONE GETS IT.
YOU'RE WELCOME, BY THE WAY.

BWAHAHAHAHA
YOU DORKS JUST GAVE US A FREE PASS TO RUN WILD!
LOOK OUT WORLD! THE BADDEST BOYS ARE *BACK!*
SO... BACK IN JAIL BY THE END OF THE DAY?
IF THEY DON'T GET LOST IN THE MINES.

HOW ARE YOU HANDLING SONIC BEING... Y'KNOW...?
I'M FINE.

I MEAN IT, LITTLE DUDE.
ME TOO. AND IT'S GOING TO BE OKAY, I PROMISE.

I'M SURE WE'LL SEE SONIC AGAIN ONE DAY. HE'S BEATEN THE ODDS A MILLION TIMES AND...
...I BELIEVE IN HIM. BECAUSE HE'S NEVER LET ME DOWN.

AND UNTIL THEN, HE'LL BE COUNTING ON US TO KEEP THE PEACE.
??
I CAN SEE WHY HE'S ALWAYS HANGING OUT WITH YOU. YOU'RE ACES!

AWW! THANKS!
OF COURSE!
AND SONIC WOULD EXPECT US TO CELEBRATE US SURVIVING!
PARTY'S AT MY PLACE! AND EVERYONE IS INVITED!

"TOO BAD SILVER'S ALREADY GONE HOME!"
THE FUTURE.
WELL... I'M BACK TO MY OWN TIME PERIOD. THE GRASS IS NORMAL. THAT'S... A GOOD SIGN.
BUT A LOT CAN CHANGE IN A COUPLE HUNDRED YEARS. IS EVERYTHING RESTORED, OR...?
SONIC... EVERYONE... *THANK YOU*. WE MADE A GOOD FUTURE.

DR. EGGMAN'S LAB-- THE PRESENT.
"MAY YOUR TIME STAY PEACEFUL, TOO."
EGG-V0678
AND NOW FOR THE FINISHING TOUCH!
HOW DOES IT FEEL TO BE CORPOREAL AGAIN, OMEGA?
GOOD. DESTROYING YOU WILL ENHANCE THIS BY 90%.
WOO-HA-HA-HA! OH, I BET IT WOULD! BUT I LOCKED DOWN YOUR BODY, SO THERE WILL BE NO MAYHEM FOR YOU!
SATISFACTION DECREASED BY 100%.
IT GETS BETTER! I'LL BE USING YOU FOR A SPECIAL PROJECT.
WELCOME BACK TO THE EGGMAN EMPIRE, E-123!
HATRED PROCESSING AT PEAK EFFICIENCY!

ORBOT! CUBOT! REPORT!
NO GOOD NEWS I'M AFRAID, BOSS.
THE ZOMBOTS REALLY DID A NUMBER ON YOUR BASES, ESPECIALLY ONCE THE DEADLY SIX TOOK OVER.
WHERE ARE THOSE MISERABLE ZETI, ANYWAY?
ZAVOK WAS DEFEATED AND HAS BEEN SAFELY LOCKED AWAY.
THE OTHER FIVE ARE AT LARGE BUT APPEAR TO BE LAYING LOW.

THERE'S NOTHING FOR IT, THEN. IT'S FULL STEAM AHEAD ON THE NEXT PROJECT!
GEE, BOSS, WHY NOT TAKE A VACATION?
INDEED. YOU WORKED VERY HARD TRYING TO DOOM US ALL.
AND I KNOW I'D LIKE SOME TIME OFF.
YEAH! GO SOME PLACE NICE. LIKE THE BASEMENT!
KEEP DREAMING BIG, BUDDY.
THIS IS NO TIME TO REST. I NEED TO ESTABLISH MY NEXT PLAN BEFORE SONIC INEVITABLY RETURNS TO CAUSE ME HEADACHES.
AND NOW I HAVE TO FACTOR IN THE ERRANT ZETI. THE CACOPHONIC CONCH WAS LOST WHEN ROUGE CRASHED THE FACESHIP, WHICH LEAVES ME DEFENSELESS AGAINST THEM.
AND THERE'S DR. STARLINE TO CONSIDER...
WHATEVER HAPPENED TO YOUR FANBOY-- I MEAN-- PROTEGE?
OH, YEAH! I LIKED HIM! HE SMELLED NICE.
THAT'S THE THING-- I DON'T KNOW.
HE OPENED A WARP PORTAL, AND I PUNTED HIM THROUGH IT. I DIDN'T THINK TO LOOK WHERE HE WAS RETREATING TO.

"HE COULD BE ANYWHERE."
DR. STARLINE'S REPOSITORY.
OH, DOCTOR... WHY CAN'T YOU SEE THE ERROR IN YOUR WAYS?

EGGMAN TRULY IS THE GENIUS I THOUGHT HIM TO BE, BUT HE'S INEPT IN HIS EXECUTION!
AND SONIC IS EVERY BIT THE POWERHOUSE I EXPECTED, BUT HE'S JUST... RECKLESS!

SO MUCH WASTED POTENTIAL. BUT I HAVE THE CLARITY OF VISION. I CAN... IMPROVE UPON THEM.

FEAR NOT, DOCTOR. I AM STILL LOYAL, DESPITE YOUR CRUELTY.
I'LL CONQUER THE WORLD. SURPASS YOU SO THAT YOU MIGHT LEARN BY EXAMPLE.

AND WHEN I SEAT YOU ON THE THRONE OF VICTORY, YOU WILL ACKNOWLEDGE I WAS RIGHT.
YOU WILL LISTEN TO ME. AND WE WILL WORK TOGETHER AS EQUAL MINDS.

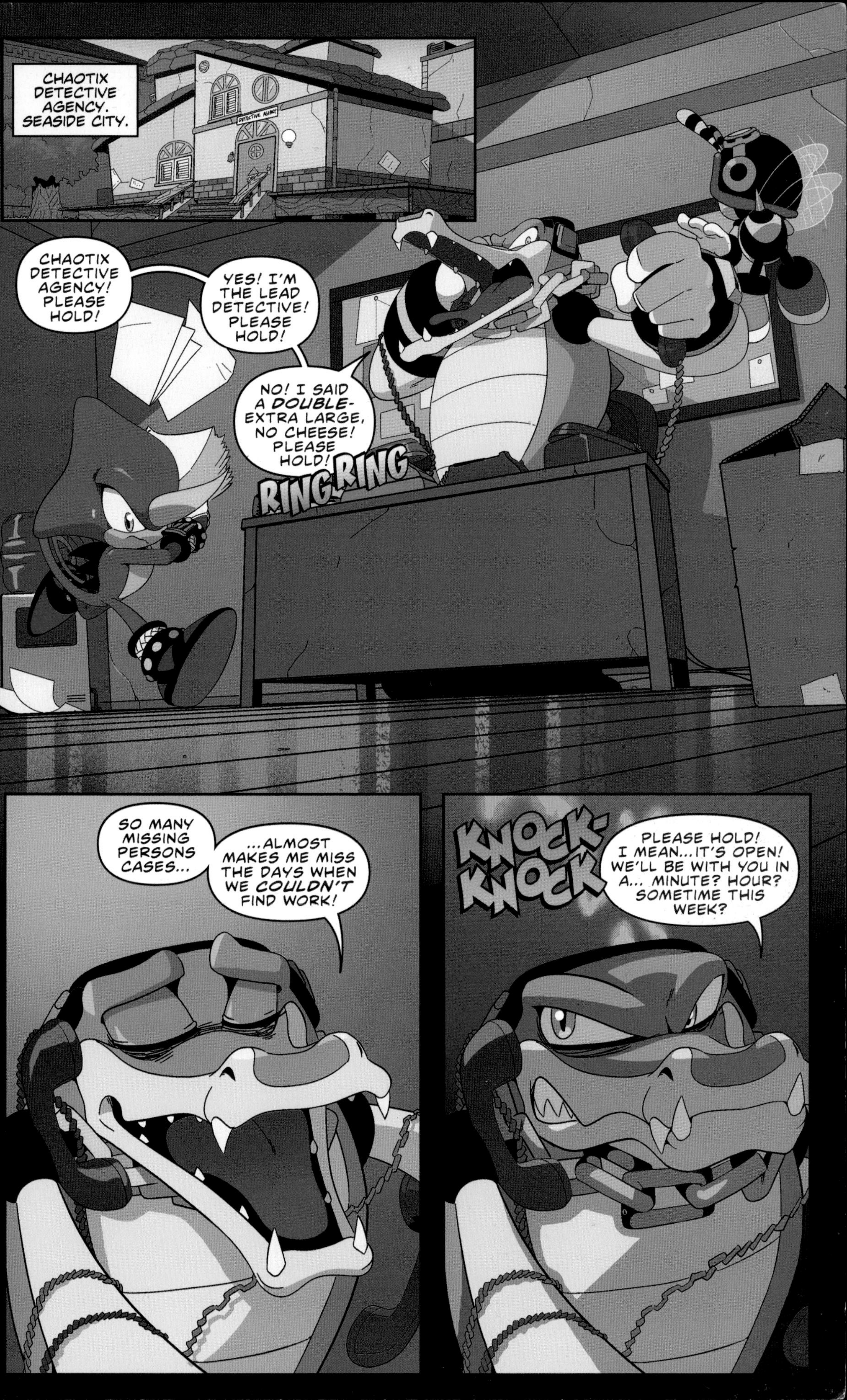
CHAOTIX DETECTIVE AGENCY. SEASIDE CITY.
DETECTIVE AGENCY
CHAOTIX DETECTIVE AGENCY! PLEASE HOLD!
YES! I'M THE LEAD DETECTIVE! PLEASE HOLD!
NO! I SAID A DOUBLE-EXTRA LARGE, NO CHEESE! PLEASE HOLD!
RING RING
SO MANY MISSING PERSONS CASES...
...ALMOST MAKES ME MISS THE DAYS WHEN WE COULDN'T FIND WORK!
KNOCK-KNOCK
PLEASE HOLD! I MEAN...IT'S OPEN! WE'LL BE WITH YOU IN A... MINUTE? HOUR? SOMETIME THIS WEEK?

HELLO, EVERYONE!
YOU'VE BEEN WORKING SO HARD TO REUNITE EVERYONE AND THEIR FAMILIES! SO WE BROUGHT YOU LOTS OF TASTY TREATS TO KEEP YOU GOING!

YOU ARE A TREASURE, MISS CREAM.
OOOOOH! GIMME!

EVEN AT THE HEIGHT OF THE PLAGUE, YOU WERE ALL SO SELFLESS.
OH! WELL! I-IT'S ALL PART OF BEING A GOOD DETECTIVE, MA'AM.
PLEASE! CALL ME VANILLA.

O-OKAY!

RING
RING
RING

SORRY, VANILLA, BUT WE DON'T HAVE TIME TO EAT. OR SLEEP. OR DO OUR JOB, IRONICALLY.
RING RING RING

WELL THAT SIMPLY WON'T DO. GEMERL, WOULD YOU MIND HELPING?
AT ONCE. SCANNING DATA. PREPARING A DATABASE OF ALL MISSING PERSONS.

CHEESE? CHOCOLA? PUT THE FILES AWAY PLEASE?
CREAM AND I WILL HANDLE THE CALLS FOR NOW AND UPDATE YOU AS GEMERL PROCESSES INFORMATION.
I'LL TAKE LOTS OF NOTES!
SO THAT MEANS...

...WE'RE FREE TO DO OUR THING! *LET'S GO, CHAOTIX!*

FOREST HILL.
"TIME TO FIND THOSE MISSING PEOPLE!"
THERE YOU ARE!
YOU CAN BE A PAIN TO TRACK DOWN, Y'KNOW?
THINGS SEEMED TO HAVE SETTLED DOWN.
ALL THE BAD GUYS ARE IN HIDING. AT LEAST THEY'RE NOT CAUSING TROUBLE.
BUT... I CAN'T FIND ANY SIGN OF SONIC OR OMEGA.
DID YOU HEAR A WORD I SAID?
YES.
WHAT'S UP? YOU'RE EVEN MORE BROODING THAN USUAL.

HE SAID TO RUN. WHAT I THOUGHT WAS COWARDICE WAS A WARNING. THAT ONE MISTAKE TOOK ME OUT OF THE FIGHT.
ME--THE *ULTIMATE LIFE-FORM*--MISCALCULATING LIKE THAT...
...IT'S UNACCEPTABLE!
IF YOU CAN'T TALK ABOUT IT, I'LL LEAVE IT BE.
I OWE HIM. NOW HE'S GONE. THAT'S ALL.

THERE'S A BIG PARTY GOING DOWN AT SPIRAL HILL TONIGHT. EVERYONE'S INVITED--EVEN YOU.
PASS.
FIGURED, BUT I THOUGHT I'D TRY.

SPIRAL HILL VILLAGE.

WHERE'S MY ICE SCULPTURE? I NEARLY GOT INFECTED TO SAVE YOU INGRATES! WHERE'S MY RECOGNITION?!

DINNER, AND A SHOW.
WE OUGHTA SAVE THE WORLD MORE OFTEN!

SIMMER, GIRL.
THEY ATTACKED THE TOWN.
YEAH, BUT THEY DID HELP SAVE US ALL. LET'S GIVE 'EM THIS ONE.

PLUS I'D RATHER NOT HAVE ANOTHER FIGHT IN MY HOME TOWN SO SOON, Y'KNOW?
I UNDER-STAND.
THAT'S MY GIRL! NOW LET'S GET SOME GRUB FOR YOUR WISPS!
THEY DO EAT, RIGHT?

MWA-HA-HA-HA! THE LIFE OF THE PARTY'S HERE!
YOU GOTTA BE KIDDIN' ME!

AND I'LL BE ENDING ALL OF YOURS!

ART BY **ADAM BRYCE THOMAS**

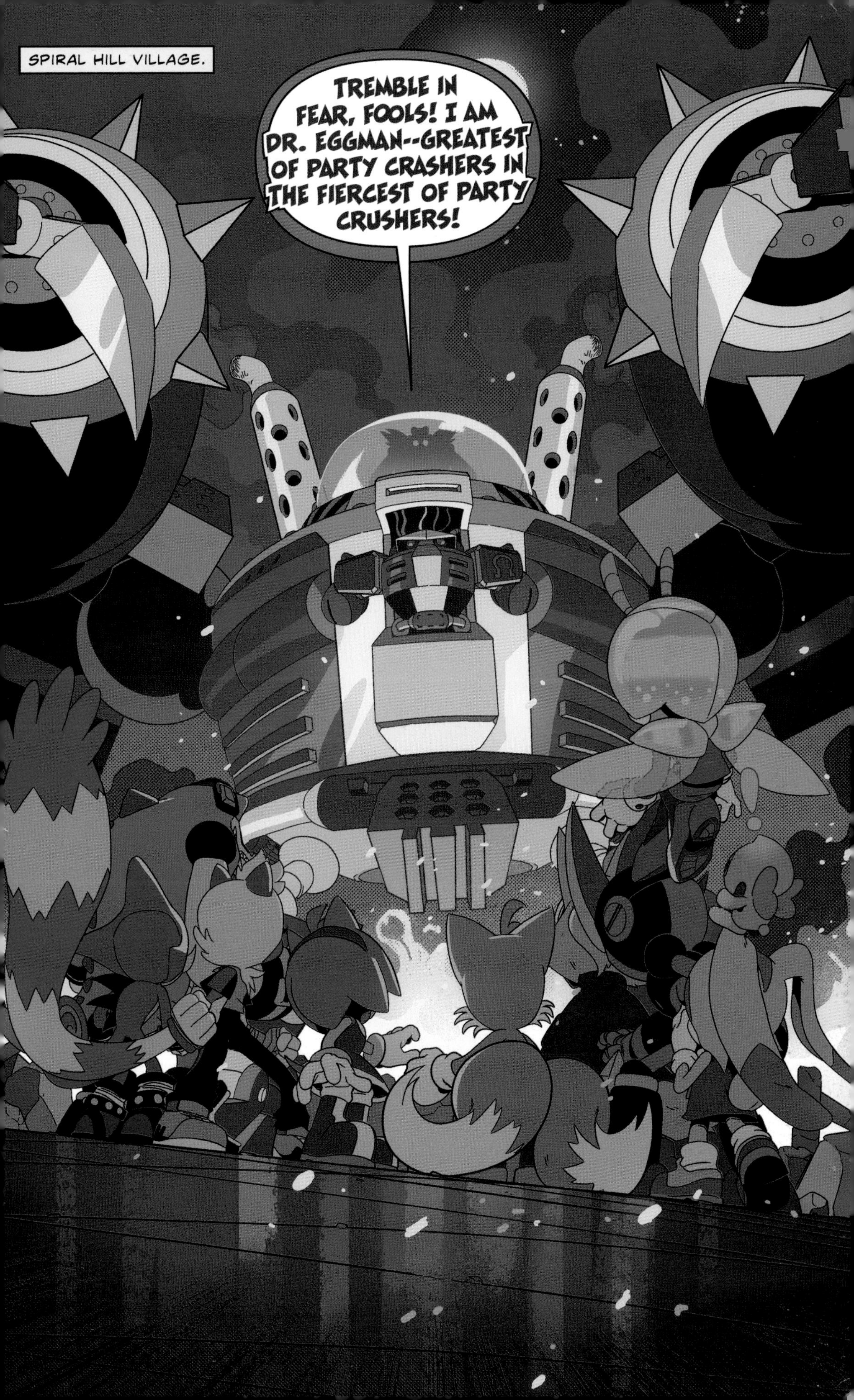
SPIRAL HILL VILLAGE.
TREMBLE IN FEAR, FOOLS! I AM DR. EGGMAN--GREATEST OF PARTY CRASHERS IN THE FIERCEST OF PARTY CRUSHERS!

I SIMPLY MUST THANK YOU FOR GATHERING TOGETHER IN ONE PLACE!
IT MAKES DESTROYING YOU ALL SO MUCH EASIER!
AMY. ORDERS?
I'M NOT LEADING THE RESTORATION ANYMORE.
I PASSED IT OFF TO JEWEL.
JEWEL. ORDERS?
I DON'T KNOW! I'M JUST HANDLING THE PAPERWORK! YOU'RE ALL THE HERO-TYPES!
WHAT'S THE CALL, JET?
WHAT DO YOU THINK?

FROGGY? WHERE ARE YOU?
WE ALREADY HELPED THESE JERKS ONCE.
LET THEM HANDLE EGGMAN WHILE WE HELP OURSELVES TO THE GEMS AND GET OUTTA HERE!

TAILS! USE YOUR COMPUTER THINGY AND TRY TO MESS WITH THE MECHA'S PROGRAMMING!
CUSTOM CODING, COMING UP!
FLYING GUYS! TRY TO BUST INTO THE COCKPIT!
THE REST OF YOU ARE WITH ME!
AIM FOR THE LEG JOINTS AND BRING HIM DOWN!
WHERE ARE ALL THE GEMS?!
IT'LL HURT RETURNING THESE, BUT IT'S WORTH IT JUST FOR THIS MOMENT.

YOU WILL NOT MENACE CREAM FURTHER!
GEMERL! BE CAREFUL!
FRIP
FRIP
FRIP
BWA-HA-HA-HA!
THAT'S TWO WAYWARD CREATIONS BACK UNDER MY CONTROL! NOW I HAVE TWICE THE COMBAT CODING AND PROCESSING POWER--A QUADRUPLE POWER-UP OVERALL!
SO THANKS FOR THE UPGRADE!
FWEEEEEE
ZAP
BLAM

IMPERIAL PALACE OF THE SOL EMPIRE. BLAZE'S WORLD & DIMENSION.
HOW ARE YOU THIS EVENING... "MR. NEEDLE-MOUSE?"
OH, HELLO, YOUR HIGHNESS. JUST TAKING A BRIEF JOG--A FEW LAPS--AROUND THE ISLAND ON THIS LOVELY EVENING.
AT LEAST HE'S STILL RUNNING AROUND...
TRULY.
WHILE I AGREE WE MUST DO ANYTHING TO HELP HIM, ARE YOU SURE THIS WILL WORK?
NO. THE NATURE OF SONIC'S ARRIVAL, HIS MEMORY LOSS, ARE ALL A MYSTERY. ANYTHING WE ATTEMPT WILL HAVE A DEGREE OF UNCERTAINTY TO IT.
BUT I HAVE FAITH IN THE POWER OF THE ***SOL EMERALDS***. AND AS THEIR GUARDIAN, ONLY I MAY USE THEIR POWER FOR THIS TASK.

SONIC.
YOU KEEP CALLING ME THAT, BUT-- OH, MY.
MAY THE POWER OF THE SOL EMERALDS HELP YOU TO REMEMBER!
GAZE INTO THE SACRED FIRE AND HAVE IT FUEL THE WINDS OF YOUR SPIRIT!
RECALL OUR PAST ADVENTURES! RECALL ALL THE GOOD YOU HAVE DONE!
RETURN TO US! RETURN TO THE HERO I KNOW YOU TO BE!
WHAT ARE YOU TALKING ABOUT? WHY ARE YOU ON FIRE?! AND WHY--
--WHY IS IT SO FAMILIAR...?

SPIRAL HILL VILLAGE. SONIC'S WORLD & DIMENSION.
SO THIS IS NEW AND TERRIBLE. GOT A PLAN, SWEETIE?
I'VE WRITTEN SOME CODE THAT SHOULD INTERFERE WITH THAT THING'S SYSTEMS AND EJECT GEMERL, BUT THERE'S NO WIRELESS RECEIVER!
I'LL NEED A HARD LINE TO UPLOAD IT!
WELL, BREAKING-AND-ENTERING IS SORT OF MY THING. TELL ME WHEN YOU'RE READY TO GO.
LOOK FOR AN ACCESS PANEL ON THE BACK IN THREE... TWO... ONE...
GO!
CONSTRUCTION ON THIS IS PRETTY SHODDY. THE DOCTOR THREW THIS TOGETHER IN A HURRY.
SO HE PROBABLY DIDN'T DO MUCH TO HIDE--
--EUREKA!

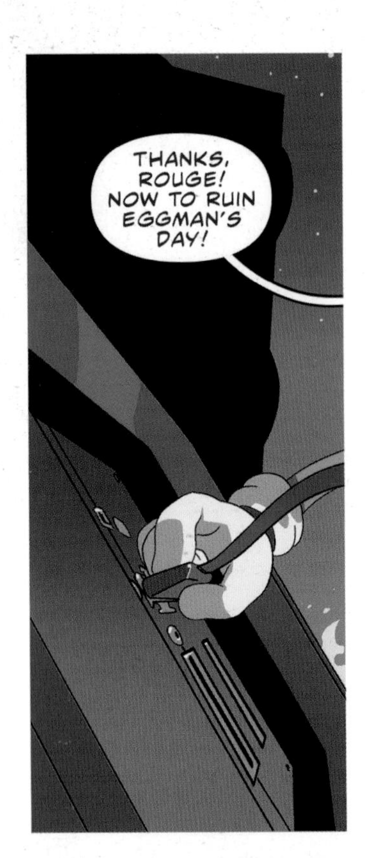
THANKS, ROUGE! NOW TO RUIN EGGMAN'S DAY!

ZORCH

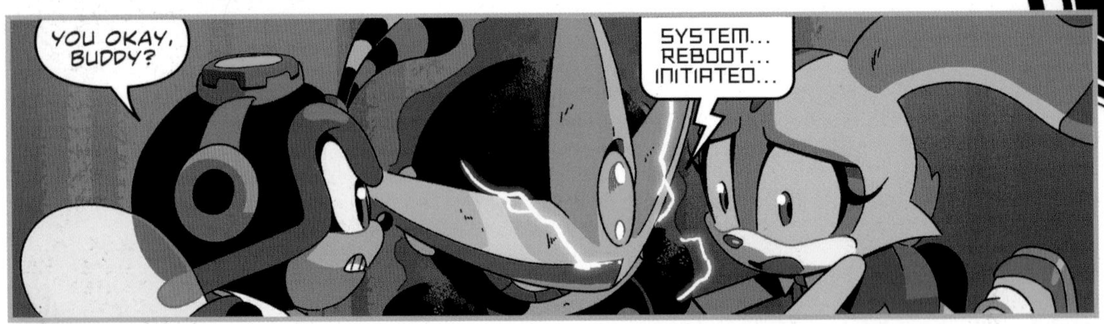
YOU OKAY, BUDDY?
SYSTEM... REBOOT... INITIATED...

HEY! THAT'S NOT JUST A WEIRD COSMETIC CHOICE! OMEGA IS LITERALLY PART OF THIS THING!
WELL, GET HIM OUT!
I'M WORKING ON IT! BUT HE'S HARDWIRED INTO THE CHASSIS. I'LL SEE IF THERE'S AN EJECTION PROTOCOL...

HACK INTO MY SYSTEMS, WILL HE?!

POW
GET DOWN!

PRIMARY SYSTEMS ONLINE. SECONDARY PROGRAMMING ACTIVE.

MUST DESTROY EGGMAN! MUST... DESTROY... EGGMAN'S... ENEMIES!
WARNING! CASCADE ERROR!
SO MUCH TO SHOOT! TOO CONFLICTED TO AIM!

THE BARRAGE HAS STOPPED... HE'S STUCK! LET'S GET HIM WHILE WE CAN!

BONK
SHUNK
BAH! I'VE TOYED WITH YOU FOOLS LONG ENOUGH!

OMEGA! BACK ON YOUR LEASH!
TACKITY-TACKITY-TACKITY

C'MON! FIGHT HIM!
SYSTEM... OVERRIDE...

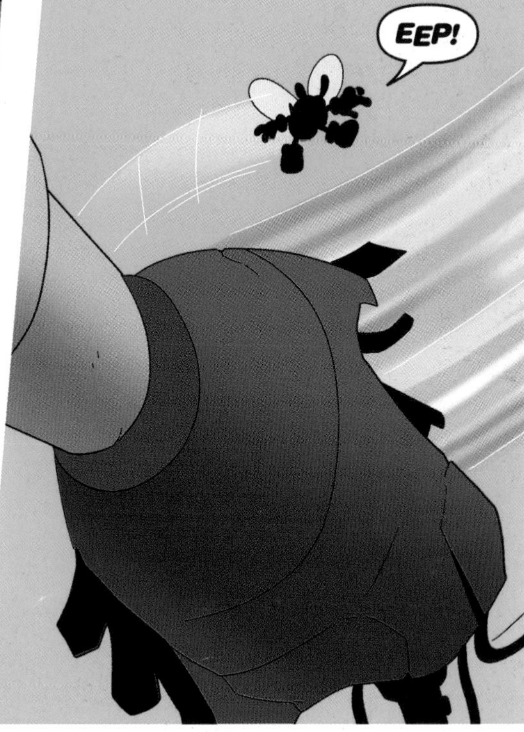
EEP!

HOW DO YOU FEEL NOW?
...SONIC?
LIKE I DID ONE TOO MANY LOOP-DE-LOOPS IN A ROW. BUT *DEFINITELY* A LOT LESS WARPED.
THANKS FOR PUTTING CHILI BACK ON MY DOG, BLAZE.
I'M JUST HAPPY TO HAVE YOU BACK TO YOUR OLD SELF.
CAN YOU REMEMBER IF YOUR WORLD IS ALL RIGHT?
IT'S FUZZY BUT... YEAH. THINGS WERE DICEY, BUT SILVER AND I HANDLED IT.
AND IN "HANDLING IT," YOU CRASH-LANDED IN MY GARDEN WITH AMNESIA.
HEH, WELL... YOU KNOW ME. I LIKE TO MAKE AN ENTRANCE.
SORRY, BY THE WAY.

NOT TO SOUND UNGRATEFUL, BUT I DIDN'T EXACTLY SAY "GOOD-BYE" BEFORE LEAVING.
EVERYBODY MUST BE WORRIED.
CAN YOU SEND ME HOME?
OF COURSE.
PLEASE GIVE MY BEST TO AMY AND CREAM.
WILL DO. BUT COME VISIT SOON, OKAY?
WE ALL MISS HAVING YOU AROUND.
THANK YOU. I WILL.
BWOOSH

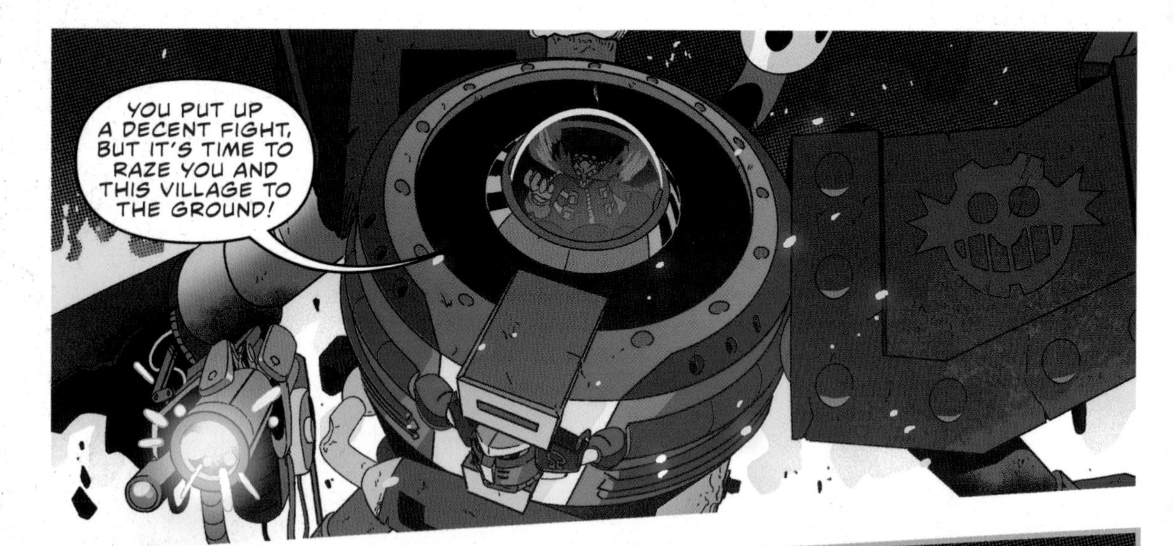
YOU PUT UP A DECENT FIGHT, BUT IT'S TIME TO RAZE YOU AND THIS VILLAGE TO THE GROUND!

OH, *NOW* WHAT?!
BWOOSH
HEY, GUYS. MISS ME?

LOOKS LIKE I'M UNFASHIONABLY LATE. WHAT'S THE SITCH, LI'L BRO?
EGGMAN IS USING OMEGA AS THE CORE FOR THE BIGGER MECHA!
GOT IT!
NO NO NO!!!
I HAD THEM! I'D WON!
WHAM
WHAM
WHAM
WHAM
OUT... YOU... GO!
UNLEASHING STOCKPILED WRATH!

BRAKKA-RAKKA-RAKKA
AMMO DEPLETED.
S'ALL GOOD, MAN. YOU DID YOUR PART.
DO NOT PATRONIZE ME.
YOU JUST COULDN'T STAY GONE, COULD YOU?! JUST HAD TO COME BACK AND RUIN MY FUN!
ALWAYS, EGG-FACE. ANYTIME. ANYWHERE.
COME A LITTLE CLOSER. WE'LL GO ANOTHER ROUND.

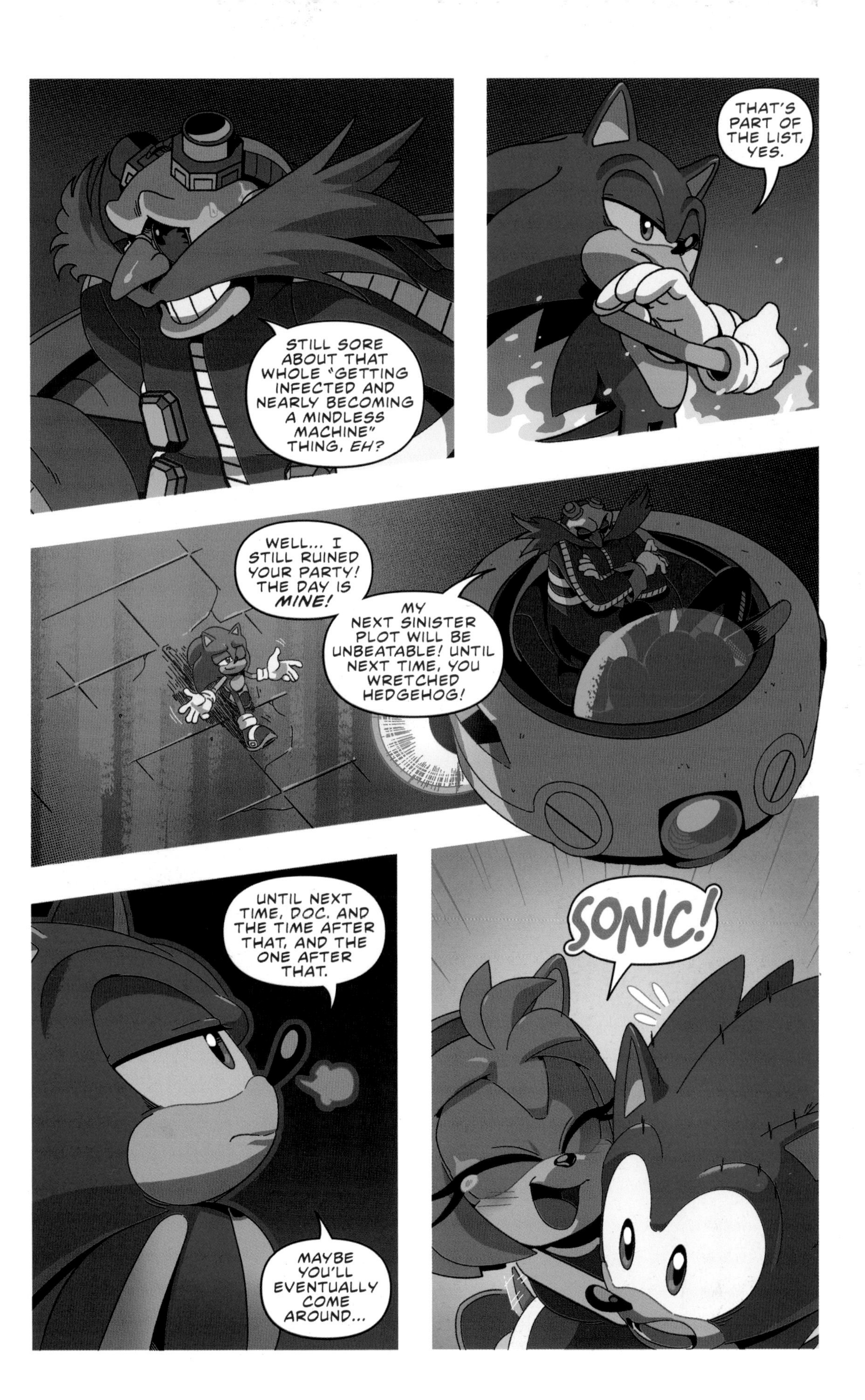
STILL SORE ABOUT THAT WHOLE "GETTING INFECTED AND NEARLY BECOMING A MINDLESS MACHINE" THING, EH?
THAT'S PART OF THE LIST, YES.
WELL... I STILL RUINED YOUR PARTY! THE DAY IS MINE!
MY NEXT SINISTER PLOT WILL BE UNBEATABLE! UNTIL NEXT TIME, YOU WRETCHED HEDGEHOG!
UNTIL NEXT TIME, DOC. AND THE TIME AFTER THAT, AND THE ONE AFTER THAT.
MAYBE YOU'LL EVENTUALLY COME AROUND...
SONIC!

I WAS WORRIED WE'D NEVER SEE YOU AGAIN!
AWW... IT WAS JUST A LITTLE CATACLYSMIC, REALITY-BENDING EXPLOSION. I WAS *FINE*.
BLAZE SAYS "HEY," BY THE WAY.
I KNEW YOU'D BE BACK! *I KNEW IT!*

YO! ARE WE GETTING OUR VICTORIOUS GROUP HUG ON?
YOU KNOW IT!
YEAH! EVERYBODY GETS IN ON THIS!

TANGLE...
WHOOPS! MISSED YOU! I THINK YOU CAN WEDGE IN HERE BETWEEN ME AND SONIC!
I HATE TO RUIN THE MOOD, BUT...

...THE TOWN IS STILL ON FIRE.

EASILY FIXED. YOUR TOWN IS REALLY INVASION-PRONE, Y'KNOW THAT?
I'LL HAVE YOU KNOW WE WERE PERFECTLY BORING UNTIL YOU SHOWED UP, MISTER!
HAHA! LET'S GO!

HE NEVER STOPS, DOES HE?
NOPE! AND NEITHER SHOULD WE-- COME ON!

IT'S GOOD TO BE BACK. GOOD TO BE HEALTHY.
I HOPE SILVER AND BLAZE CAN COME BACK AND NOT HAVE TO DEAL WITH SOME KIND OF DISASTER.
A NEW DAY MEANS NEW ADVENTURES! SO NO MORE LYING AROUND...
...TIME TO FIND OUT WHAT COMES NEXT!

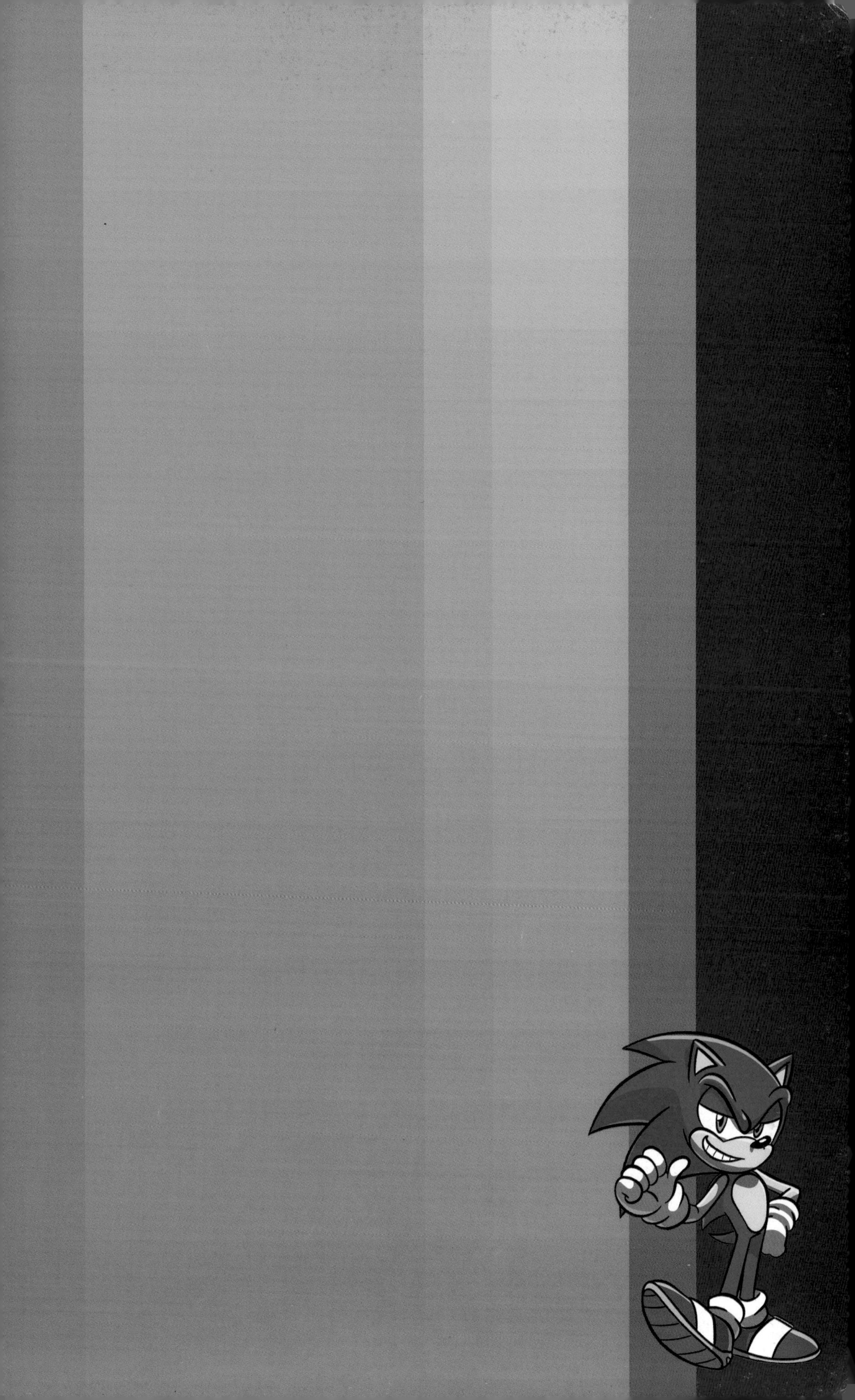

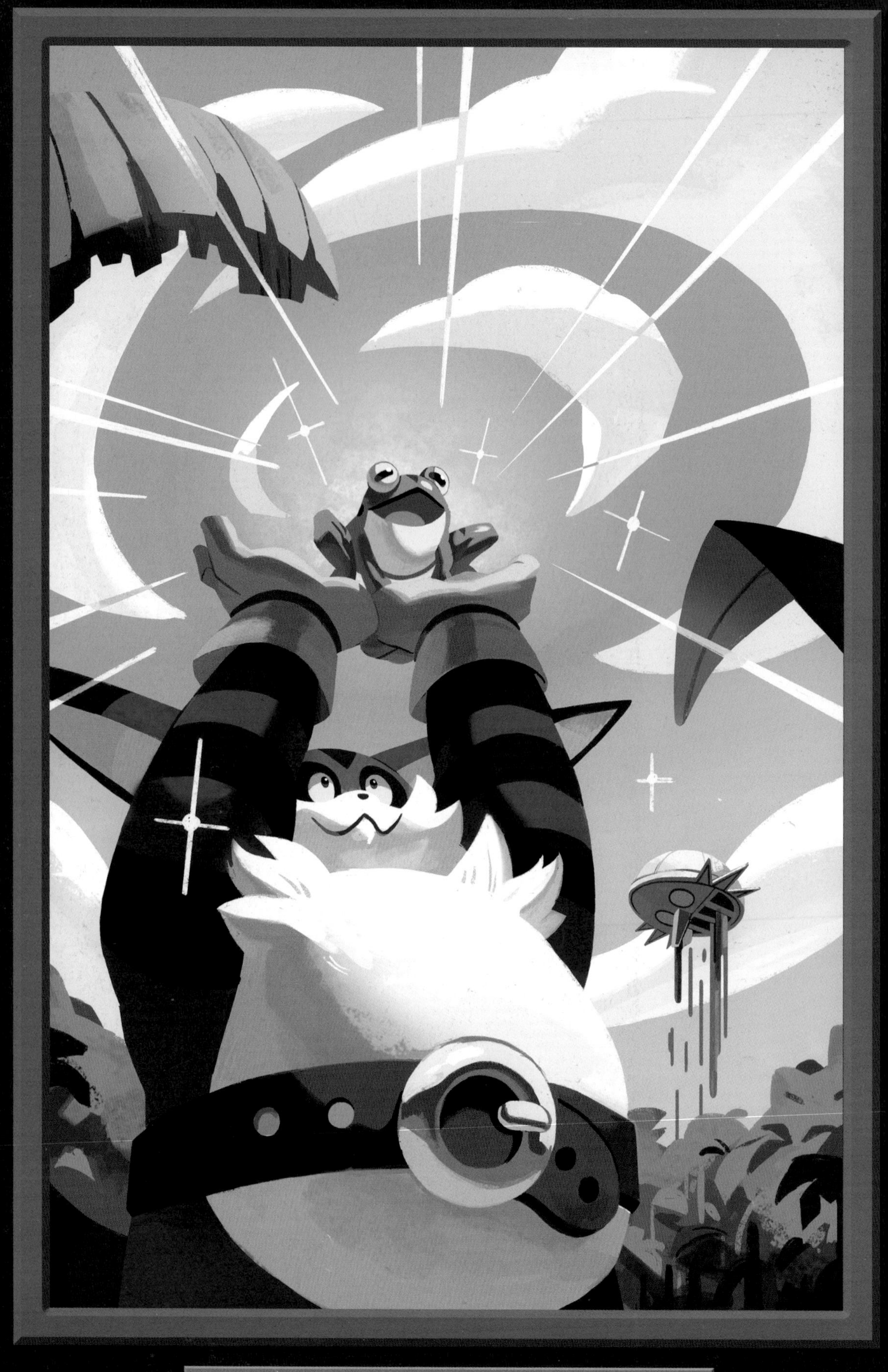

ART BY **NATHALIE FOURDRAINE**

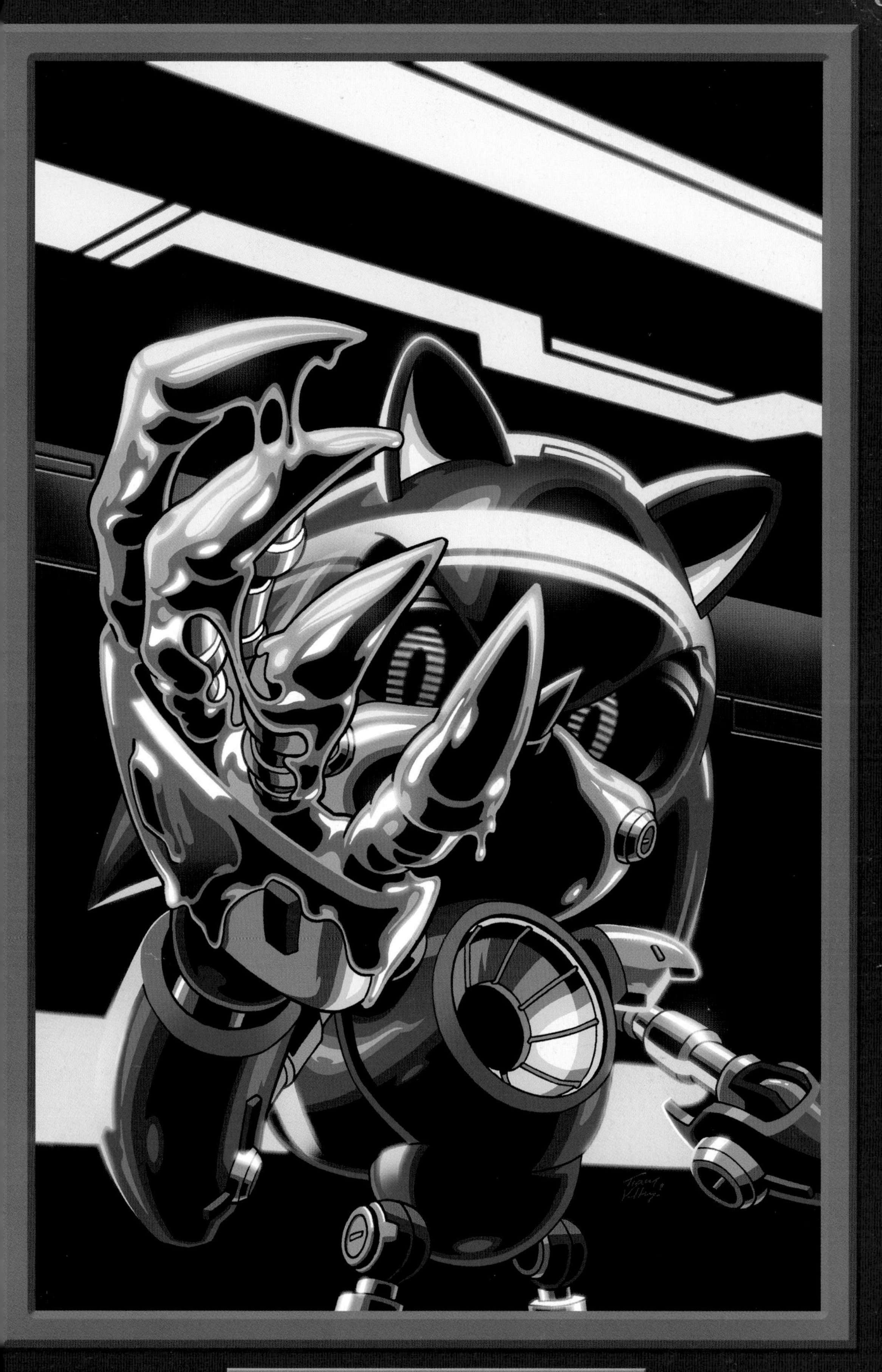

ART BY **TRACY YARDLEY**

ART BY **REGGIE GRAHAM**

ART BY **DIANA SKELLY**

ITO

ART BY **NATHALIE FOURDRAINE**

ART BY **NATHALIE FOURDRAINE**